THE PRETZEL-BENDERS

Book #1

by

Medo H. Maz

To P.V. So far on from that dark and bizarre, yet enlightening past, you were right. Even paths drawn with squiggly lines can lead to meaningful purpose.

Pretzel-bender: A peculiar person; an eccentric; one who thinks in a round-about manner.

1

THE NEWCOMER

CHAPTER ONE

Everything in Joseph's body shook. Every bone, muscle, and connective tissue trembled as a hot, intense wave of stress surged through his veins. He was carried away from the vehicle, unsure if the body beneath the coat on the front passenger seat was his mother. He could no more control the tears pouring down his face or the screams bursting out of his mouth, than one could control the heaving convulsions of uncontrollable vomiting. Every molecule in him told him his mother was dead.

The only silver lining in Joseph's moment of devastation was the luck of being so young and absent-minded that he didn't question the bulging coat hanging over the seat in front of him or the growing malodor in the car. He didn't even consider that his mom was on the precipice of death the moment he entered the car, let alone that she was there at all. Not until the sound of her last breath exited her body and pierced his heart like a bundle of titanium needles.

As one of his mother's associates carried him away from the car kicking and screaming over his shoulder, a pair of cold metallic arms extended from a large machine and began lifting the car off the ground. Joseph fell silent with numbing immediacy. The hot wave blowing through his veins was replaced with a harsh menacing pressure biting down on his veins like a snake mistaking a garden hose for its prey.

As the car rose higher towards the machine's gaping mouth, Joseph was suddenly facing away from the car as the man carrying him turned around. Like a switch, Joseph's tears and roaring scream burst out of him, causing the other man standing a few feet away to flinch.

"Let her out!" Joseph demanded, squirming violently.

He caught the two men glancing at each other and shrugging.

The man carrying him grunted in pain as Joseph struck his kidney with a sharp kick. The man shouted obscenities as his arm loosened, letting Joseph slide awkwardly off his back and onto the cold rocky ground beneath him just as the sound of metal crashing against metal echoed in the air. Ignoring his own pain from landing onto the harsh ground with his hands, Joseph turned and began to run in the direction of the daunting machine playing the ill-suited role of his mother's casket, but quickly felt himself taken by the waist followed by a prick in his neck sending him into an overwhelming state of fatigue followed by darkness.

Joseph wasn't sure how long he was out for, but he could just about feel the warmth of his eyelids again as he slowly awoke. However, not much sense followed. He could just about muster his right eyelids open to a miniscule degree but enough to tell that he was inside a nice car given how wide the beige seats he was lying horizontally on were along with the sensation of warm, supple, buttery-smooth leather against his cheek. The only unwelcome disturbance was sporadic bumps in the road the car was traveling. He could just about make out two figures sitting at the front of the car. His eyelids grew heavy again, and he began to fade out of consciousness once more as a warm hand cupped his ankle.

None the wiser of how long he was out for again, Joseph regained the paltry strength to crack enough of his eyelids open to notice that he was in a bright room. A den or study of some sort given the sliver of a glossy rose-brown desk he caught in the corner of his eyes. His resting place was not as pleasant as the last. It was warm but a little harsher to the skin of his cheeks. It was a bit scratchy like his grandparents' antique floral sofa. As if his ears had been plugged shut with an air-bubble previously that finally popped, Joseph could now hear his surroundings but still struggled to crack his eyelids any wider.

There was a bludgeoning cry bouncing off the walls of the study. The cry hit heavy like a battering ram, but its vibrations brushed over him with a softness and tenderness akin to falling cherry blossom leaves kissing your cheeks as gravity carried them to your toes. Joseph turned his neck ever so slightly and saw a woman roughly around the age of his mother. The woman cried with the abandon of a child who'd fallen and scrapped their knee running around the playground. Her knees rested upon the carpeted floor, and her hands were limp by her sides with the palms of her hands facing the ceiling.

Four men hovered around her with terror strewn upon their faces as though one of them had shattered their employer's heirloom baccarat crystal vase. For the first time in what felt like an inordinate amount of time, Joseph could feel his heartbeat, and he felt it pause then skip in that moment as the pale woman with the red cheeks and blue eyes fell silent. Her eyes met his barley open eyes. She then looked away from him and at her knees as she gently wiped the tears off her face. She soon began to rub the tip of her nose with the palm of her hand while sniffling like one recovering from a sudden burst of sneezing before swiftly rising from her knees like a graceful gazelle deciding to transition from rest to activity. She lunged violently at the man next to her who bore a resemblance to the man who'd been carrying Joseph earlier.

Joseph felt a warm hand cup his ankle and dozed off again.

This time, a cold breeze caressing Joseph's nose gave him a bit of a waking jolt. Not enough to crack his eyes wide open, but enough to slightly pull both ajar. However, his visibility was poorer with a coat of moisture blurring his vision. He could feel himself carried by large, reliable arms. Regrettably, arms that didn't bother covering him from the cold winds outside biting at his fingertips and the tip of his nose. He couldn't tell much other than the warm orange glow from the streetlamps nearby and that they were in some kind of outdoor space enclosed by high fencing. The large figure carrying him had dark skin like him and his mother, he noticed. Joseph's attention was drawn away from the man carrying him to the sound of pacing footsteps against a rough pebble-covered surface. He moved his neck slightly to the side and froze at the realization that the man carrying him might have been the one who'd been sedating him every time he came to. The warm hand on his ankle the two times prior felt like a large blanket. With his neck to his side, Joseph hoped he wouldn't be sedated again.

He looked ahead and saw that woman again. Her face was too blurry to say for sure, but she seemed to be wearing the same white nightgown from earlier. She stopped pacing and began swinging something thick, long, and steely at a blurry brown object resembling a paper bag on a brown wooden fence post. She swung at it frantically, which seemed to collapse the object's top bit by bit like a soda can until it fell forward against her knees and slid to the ground. The moisture from Joseph's right eye managed to subside, and he gasped at the sight of a man with an indistinguishable collapsed face fallen at the pale woman's feet. Her lips were moving as she turned her back to the body and looked up at the clear night sky, but he couldn't hear her well enough.

"Jesus," said the man carrying Joseph.

Joseph turned his head and met the man's dark brown eyes as they fell heavily upon him. It was bedtime again.

Nothing was quite like sitting on one of the tall, velvet cushioned stools waiting for Ma to serve up a divine midafternoon snack. Joseph wasn't sure if he'd ever feel like he was home again without his mother, but he knew that he'd always feel safe in Ma's kitchen and under her roof. Her own flesh and blood with their thick, dirty brown hair and blue eyes sat on each of the stools to his right, talking over each other about every minute of Mighty Morphine Power Rangers and starting to get physically agitated about their discussion. However, they quickly fell silent as Ma opened the oven door and the scent of sweet vanilla extract and chocolate chip engulfed the kitchen, but as powerful as that aroma was, Ma's signature scent of chamomile and jasmine always managed to penetrate any clashing barrier around to hold strong in the hearts of Joseph and her boys.

Joseph felt an ache in his chest as his mother's face flashed in his eyes. He wanted to hold onto it longer, but a shove at his shoulder sent his mother's face into the recesses of his burdened mind. He turned and faced Grayson who had a mischievous smirk on his face.

"We already called dibs on the blue, green, red, and black Power Rangers, so you have to pick between the yellow or pink ones," said Grayson.

Ma cleared her throat and turned around from the stove. The sun, beaming through the bay windows behind her, cloaked her in light. Her soft peony pink smile calmed the anarchy in the veins of her boys and vanished the aching in Joseph's chest. However, such was the overwhelming reassurance of her smile that it almost felt violent. Violent enough to bury the memory of his mother so far down that the echoes of the past could never rival Ma again for his attention.

"Behave, my sweets. I better not see any rough play with your brother," said Ma, holding her gaze over her boys.

Joseph couldn't help but feel like an infant only just out of the crib the way Ma put it.

Grayson snickered.

While the kitchen was still awash with light and intoxicating blissful aromas and scents, it started to feel every bit like a sterile, inhospitable vacuum. Ma's eyes held still and coldly over her boys. Even though she didn't cast her cutting gaze over Joseph, he couldn't escape the splash of the severe, primal, predatory energy that Ma exuded, like a shark wearing human flesh.

"If I so much as see a scratch on your brother," said Ma as she stood an inch from the marble countertop and leaned forward letting her words hang in the air like scissors stuck in a ceiling inevitably bound to drop and draw blood.

Joseph shuddered as Ma slammed her fist on the counter making her oldest son, Jason, whelp as he held his hand over the cast wrapped around his knee and shin. Ma's boys were as pale as their mother, but they now looked as blue as corpses taking a nap in a morgue drawer.

"One for you, one for you, one for you... and one more for you," said Ma, pointing at each of her sons and stopping on Jason as she pointed at his cast with promise in her eyes.

Ma leaned away from the counter. She looked at Joseph, smiled, and let out a hearty giggle, and just like that, the kitchen filled up with air again, felt warm and bright again, and smelled like heaven.

Ma gestured Joseph over with a smile as she turned toward the stove. He hesitated for a moment before carefully stepping off the stool and made his way to her as her boys looked down at the marble countertop destitute and void of their prior animation. Ma sat on the kitchen floor with her legs crossed and a bowl of leftover chocolate whipped cream. She ran a spoon around the bowl and then held it in front of Joseph's chin. She put her other hand on his back, and Joseph felt her energy course into him. Her joy, her warmth, her optimism, her sureness, and her unwavering love for him.

Joseph felt a wet drop roll down his face. His eyes widened. He hadn't realized when he started tearing up. He noticed Ma's eyes growing watery as well. He looked down at the spoon and opened his mouth and suddenly found Ma raising the spoon and brushing it over his nose leaving him with a messy warm chocolate dollop. He looked at her with wide eyes and his mouth agape.

Ma began to laugh so loudly that you'd think she just witnessed a comical circus act of epic proportions. It was such an absurdly loud laugh that a stranger walking down the street opposite the tall fencing surrounding her San Francisco home would be forgiven if they raised their hands in defense. However, so nurturing and contagious were the echoes of her laugh that Joseph began to laugh as well, giving in to the pull of her will and spirit, as they stood face to face in tears and laughter.

CHAPTER TWO

Jordy rolled over and grabbed his phone from atop the stack of Maxim magazines next to his mattress as three gentle raps sounded from the door. He got on all fours and hoisted himself and his bulging midriff out of bed. He poked his nose at his armpits, struggling to not grimace, then looked down at his habitual, routine, certainly faultless biological tendency.

Three more gentle knocks came from the door.

The young man approached the door and looked through the peephole. A young fellow with a slightly lustrous dark complexion and neatly trimmed hair stood in the hallway with his eyes fixed on the peephole.

The stranger appeared somewhat nervous.

Just as he raised his hand to knock on the door again, the slightly less stiff occupant hid the bottom half of his body behind the door, unlocked it, and jabbed his head out.

"Hey."

The stranger first replied with a smile, arresting the reflection of his neighbor in his brown eyes.

"Hey. I moved in about a week ago." The young man in the hallway extended his hand.

Jordy's right hand held the door open while he continued to hide his lower half behind the door, failing to realize that it had shyly withdrawn, no more eager for the company than he was. "One sec, bud."

He shut the door briefly on the stranger. He extended his shorts away from his torso and looked down into the darkness. *All clear!* Just as he thought to open the door again, he realized that not six hours before he had been handling himself. Oh well, it was eight in the morning, and he hated early birds.

He stepped back out. "You can call me Jordy," he said, his back resting against the door as he reached out to the stranger.

"Cornelius," said the young man as he shook his neighbor's moist palm.

"A week ago, huh? Didn't hear a thing. What unit did you move into?"

"Unit Two." Cornelius pointed down the corridor.

"Nice. So, the good ol' fashioned next-door neighbor." He patted Cornelius' shoulder. "Well, don't hesitate to give me a shout if you need to borrow… a charger or whatever. Got a drawer stacked with them."

Just as Jordy was about to show Cornelius his back and shuffle back to the warmth of his blanket, he heard an "um."

"Anything else, bud?" he asked and could've sworn that for a fraction of a second Cornelius had a look of disgust about him.

"Just the most important thing." Cornelius' voice took on a sudden assured tone as he crept out of his mild hunch and appeared taller than he was seconds ago.

Jordy felt a rather confused and—he thought—quite misplaced instinct to run. The situation did not feel so grave, yet still, the itch to run persisted, but he lent it little attention.

"It's long. The hallway, you know," said Cornelius.

"Yeah, sure. It is," he concurred, unsure how long he'd have to stand out there before giving his new neighbor the 4-1-1 on how little people cared about the length of hallways.

"People make me nervous sometimes. I make myself nervous most of the time," said Cornelius, tugging at the hem of his T-shirt and then centering his collar. "You see, eventually, I'll be returning home one day, and you'll be heading out. Or you'll be returning home, and I'll be going out, and we're bound to come face to face. If I don't have this talk with the people around me, more often than not, I'll ignore them entirely, and it'll be because I'm too scared to say anything because I'm terrified that I'll be left hanging. My, *hello, good morning, good evening,* left to decay in purgatory. And it will be my fault most of the time because my voice is a bit subdued when I'm nervous." Cornelius looked at his neighbor, who stood with a rigid smile on his face, appearing unsure if he was expected to reply at all.

"So, you will always hear from me whenever we cross paths, and I'd appreciate hearing from you. Good day, Jordy," he said, sinking ever so slightly back into his involuntary hunch and speed-walking back to his apartment; the same nervous wreck Jordy remembered examining through the peephole of Unit Four.

"Good day!" said Jordy a little too loud, a little too late, afraid Cornelius hadn't heard him as he returned to Unit Two. Confused by why he was afraid at all.

The door to Unit Three slowly creaked open, just as it was certain the fellow from Two was nowhere in sight. A petite young lady with thick black hair and a ghostly complexion, wearing a black hoodie twice her size, peeked out at Jordy. He stood there as if entranced by the hallway, only for the poorly maintained hinges of her door to shake him out of it. He looked at her just as she formed brackets on either side of her mouth with her hands.

"What the fuck?!" she whispered. She must have suffered a similar encounter with Cornelius not long before.

Jordy shrugged and threw his hands over his shoulders as his mouth melted into a frown. He, indeed, had no idea 'what the fuck' had just happened.

The door-lock of Unit Two clicked, and the lady slammed her door shut faster than a lubed eel could slip away from the keen jaws of awkward death.

Jordy rushed into his apartment, shaking the ground for a moment, and locked the door. He then buried his head into one of the kitchen cabinets in search of the discolored Mystery Machine-inspired bong that would coax enough courage out of him to call out of work for the day.

CHAPTER THREE

Wish stood on the table. She could feel the water drying on her skin while staring over the edge, her body wrapped in a towel as her hair dried against her back. There was a minor tremor in her elbow as she held a stainless-steel frying pan over her shoulders and her eyes scoured the kitchen floor for the quick-footed spider. *This is not the day to fall behind!* her mind fretted. It was time for her to summon that false courage everyone buried deep inside and search for the awful creature that was surely more afraid of her than she was of it.

Just as Wish became resolved enough to step off the table, the fist-sized, eight-legged horror-show emerged from behind the stove and nestled itself in the farthest corner of the granite counter-top by the wall outlet. *This is it!* she thought. For the rest of her life, she'd stand frozen on the damn table to accomplish nothing other than the fear of her crawling foe. If she'd only learned the shrewd art of knife-throwing, her life wouldn't have gone to waste. She would've spent the better part of a decade growing in esteem as Berkeley's leading medical examiner before the SFPD came calling for her sharp mind and indelible leadership.

Somewhere in there, her keen mind might've drawn the attention of a shrewd psychopath with whom she would've developed a dangerous cat-and-mouse rivalry that would've intertwined her path with that of her destined lover. Perhaps a bookish detective or fireman—God forbid a lawyer in a dull monochrome suit. A man in uniform who did stuff in his uniform other than sit behind a desk and shop lumbar support cushions.

Who knows how they'd cross paths, but they would. Her Vietnamese good looks and his uncanny resemblance to Don Cheadle would undoubtedly draw them together at first, but it is the quickness and sharpness of their minds that would stir the fiery passion between them as they coalesced into a brilliant bundle of black and white tinder.

The spider suddenly shifted away from its corner and halted several feet beneath her chin on the kitchen floor, drawing her away from her fantasy. A sadist, it must have been, killing her dreams, feeding on her fear, and relishing the sight of her trembling elbow with its many eyes.

Fuck it, this is not the end! her mind bellowed.

"Ahhh!" she let out her war cry. She forgot how long she had remained motionless, as her legs felt numb, and she found herself clumsily slipping off the table and falling towards the slimy pincers of her opponent.

Wish's elbows stung as she rolled over, with the crunching sound of the six-eyed nightmare beneath the frying pan stirring last night's pho in her stomach. She groaned as she got up, the back of her head still smarting from its collision with the tiled kitchen floor. She looked to her side at the frying pan and the remains of the eight-legged ball of fuzz mushed beneath it.

She could cut open a cadaver and pull out and weigh every last organ from the rotting human cauldron, but this? This was too much.

CHAPTER FOUR

With the turn of a key and the sound of his father's footsteps growing distant, it was as if a curse had been lifted and the air was easier to breathe. They were truly home now. Charles could hear his mother's footsteps tap gently against the floor as she got out of bed, went into the kitchen, and ducked under the sink to retrieve her jar of goodies.

He pulled his blanket in tighter around himself and relished its warmth, despite knowing that in five minutes his mother would enter his room, wake him up, and help ready him for another day of summer school—with double-decker moon pies and Hershey kisses lingering on her breath.

They walked hand in hand down Prince Street, little Charles bathed and scrubbed clean, a zesty coconut scent trailing him, as his hair—over-groomed, with the sheen of polished Calacatta marble—received the wind with panache. His mother's face— as it often did—illuminated the day of every passerby with its singular brand of delicate despair. Her perfect little nose, smoother than aged Brie, and her eyes, bluer than the crystals her husband hid beneath the floorboards. Her face, frost-kissed, so nearly translucent, that one would be forgiven if they'd been tempted to cup it between their hands and believed for a moment that they could rinse themselves with its cool solitude.

She felt a sudden tug of her arm as Charles appeared to slip while she walked faster, lost in thought, forgetting that her strides were longer than his. She halted, stooped down and inspected her perfect little boy. She straightened his polo and pants, blew an eyelash off his cheek, and tightened his shoelaces.

They crossed the street two blocks and a half off Martin Luther King Jr Way and arrived at his school, where that man always waited to greet them. His mother's hand tightened around him as the man's cologne crept toward them.

"Miss Nelson. Charles. Good morning!"

Are teachers even allowed to wear that much cologne, or to be so enthused about summer school? thought Mrs. Nelson. At first, it occurred to her that Charles was perhaps struggling with math, but his progress reports to this point had shown steady improvement. Yet, the man never ceased to await them. She asked her husband if it was customary for teachers to wait outside for students, as she'd only recently started walking Charles to school, but he seemed unaware of such a thing and seemed too preoccupied to care about it. Mr. Nelson cared little for summer programs.

"I'm sorry?" the teacher said, missing what Mrs. Nelson had tried to say more clearly.

"Mrs. Nelson," she repeated, forcing a smile.

"Sorry, of course! Mrs. Nelson," he said, seeming chronically unable to remember that she was married, or more so unwilling.

"Hey, buddy." He stooped down, meeting Charles' eyes, and patted his head.

That's it! She would kill him. For every strand of her beautiful boy's hair the filthy slug unsettled, she would skin him alive, roll him in dried seeds, and cast him into a pit of fire ants.

Mrs. Nelson was afraid; she felt a strain come over her face and couldn't tell if she'd still been smiling, or if her face had contorted into a rage. She'd need to reference a mirror to be sure. She caught the man's eyes for a moment paused over her stomach before he panicked and met her gaze.

"I'll help him to class." He smiled and ran his hand through his own hair, before rising to his feet and squeezing her elbow. "You need to get to work, don't you?"

She checked her tiny wristwatch, terrified by how much time her anxieties and fantasies could kill. She turned Charles around, kissed him on the cheek, to which she caught the man moistening his lips, and tried to pat her boy's hair back into order.

Mrs. Nelson walked away, looked back at Charles once more, then left the school grounds.

CHAPTER FIVE

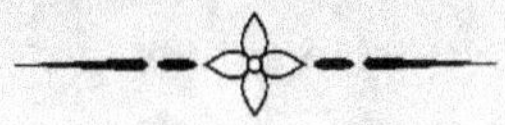

Joseph checked his watch for the third time as his behind grew numb, and his dread of the color of suit he'd chosen to wear that morning—which resembled what he'd left in the toilet not two hours before—began to fade. He took a deep breath as acceptance settled in. He was there to be judged on his salesmanship and not on his poor choice of wardrobe. At worst, he'd be advised to wear a sharper suit next time—if there was a next time—and he'd hear nothing more of it.

"Joseph?" said a bulb-shaped, red-cheeked man wearing a white shirt, dusky-blue trousers, and a sharp blue and gold necktie.

He turned and met the man's eyes.

"Come on in, son." The dealership supervisor gestured him over to his office.

Joseph took a seat in the much comfier chair across from the man and restrained himself from sighing in sweet relief as the soft cushions embraced his buns.

The man's chair squeaked as he adjusted himself to comfort and pulled a folder from his desk drawer. He looked at Joseph and smiled. Joseph could tell that despite their eyes meeting, the man was focusing on his periphery and his interviewee's hideous brown suit. The man opened the folder and pulled out what Joseph knew was his resume.

The supervisor ran his hand over his mouth, then leaned forward, before sitting back in his chair and dropping the resume on his desk.

He ran his hand over his mouth again.

"You're a seller, son, isn't that right? Your resume says as much," said the man.

"Yes, sir," replied Joseph.

"But you know what I hate?"

Joseph shook his head.

"Resumes. They don't tell you shit about the man himself. They don't tell you anything about character. I've sent four salesmen packing over the last six months. Tall, straight-jawed young gentlemen with a full head of hair, a bachelor's in business, and a good-looking resume. Problem is, not a month passes by and *they*," the veins in his neck bulged, "transfigure to *shit*!" he said, spittle stopping a centimeter short of Joseph. The redness of the man's cheeks ripened as a vein made headways to the right of his forehead.

"They couldn't sell a car if the Lord and Savior, Jesus Christ, blessed it and it shat holy water. Approached every sale like a pair of panties they were trying to fish out of Audrey Hepburn's skirt. Jesus." He turned his chair around and looked out at the large panes facing the dealership gallery.

Joseph hesitated before turning with him.

"Let me put you on the spot here. Which one of those three cars would you sell me?" he asked, poking his finger forward.

"None of them," replied Joseph without a moment's doubt.

The supervisor turned to him, the vein on his forehead growing larger with its pulse nearly visible.

"With all due respect, sir, I don't know you. And you can't sell a car to someone you don't know. I ask a potential client," said Joseph, straightening his tie and turning to face him, "I ask them about what they've driven, and what they liked and disliked about it. I want to know what they care about, what language they speak. If all they talk about is the engine, and they sound like they understand the words they're saying, then I spend one, maybe two minutes tops, talking-up tech and trims, but then we're going to get down to it—talk shop. Engine performance, horsepower, torque, suspension, and overall mechanics, until we're on the same page, and I tell them about one of the ten cars I've driven since I turned sixteen. I'm not telling them what they should jump into, going to tell them what I've jumped into. If talking shop seems intimidating to them, then I'll abridge it, and focus more on exterior design aesthetics, interior features, paintwork, and add-ons."

Joseph nudged his chair back and leaned forward, more at ease. "I can make a sale here because they aren't buying a car from a salesman. Anyone can walk into a dealership and walk out a fool—at least that's what my mother used to say. What they're doing is buying a car from a friend. And they can take that home with them and tell their family and hook up their Saturday night bar crawl pals with an Insta of them and their new wheels."

The man's vein eased, and he sighed in relief before picking the resume back up. "If you're not just a smooth talker, and you can do what you say you can do, then I'm glad to welcome you aboard, son. But I'm no fool, so you're going to have to make a friend out of me and tell me which one of those three cars you'd have me walk out of here with," he said.

Joseph grinned.

"Son!" said Jim, as Joseph was about to exit the dealership and count every second through the weekend before starting on Monday.

He turned around.

"You have a better suit at home?" Jim whispered, joining Joseph at the exit, putting his hand on his elbow and leaning in.

"Yes, sir," Joseph replied, looking worried as Jim laughed deeply, and for a moment, seemed like he was choking.

"Sorry, son." Jim wiped tears from his eyes. "Was just thinking for a moment about taking you to my mother in case you didn't have another suit. Was a master seamstress back in the day but she had to give it up once dementia settled in and she began to mistake clients for my old man, God rest his soul. Got a little grabby, she did."

It became silent.

"Well, you get old enough and you learn to laugh about everything. Now get out of here. We'll see you Monday!" He nudged Joseph out and waved goodbye as he returned to his office.

Joseph let the moment evaporate from his mind as he watched Jim disappear into his office before making his journey back to his new apartment.

CHAPTER SIX

There was a peculiar feeling whenever Wish arrived. It always felt like crossing through an invisible barrier that separated a brighter dimension from a much darker one. You felt it almost immediately, once you dipped beneath the crime-scene tape— the grotesque aura of a rotten soul.

Wish took the last shot and lifted the last set of prints before packing up. Her elbows were still sore, and her head still hummed from the morning's duel. It was never less somber; the tightness she felt around her heart whenever she finished compiling data at the scene of a crime. Berkeley wasn't heavy on murder, but near-murders were a common occurrence resulting mostly from attempted robberies and break-ins.

The mother's finger was still there, motionless by the garbage bin next to the kitchen island. Before the dark dimension had descended upon the home, it was like any other home cursed by the delusion coursing in from the brighter dimension. Bad things couldn't happen, it was simply not possible. The sun shone, so nothing bad could happen. The doors were locked, so nothing bad could happen. You could hear the kids in the playground across the street running and laughing, so no awful thing could happen. Bad people who did bad things were no different from Dementors, or Bodachs, or

Pennywise—the only reality they belonged to was in books. Unless the madness of human nature were to find itself inspired, then you'd find yourself staring into the cavernous pit-like eyes of a dark mass as it pointed your Henckels eight-inch serrated chef's knife at you, breaking the delusion that you were ever safe.

The mother said that it felt like time had stopped for a moment; that her mind would not accept what was happening as she waited for the intruder to take off his mask and joyously laugh, 'April fools!' Only, it was July. She said she thought she screamed something, though she couldn't remember what. Her daughter fumbled her phone to the ground, jumped off the stool and ran up to her room. As the culprit attempted to pursue her, the mother found herself standing between him and the stairs. He slashed at her, nicking the palm of her right hand and her chin, before lobbing off her left pinky with such force that it torpedoed into the kitchen. He then shoved past her and ran up the stairs. She found herself grappling with him on the stairs— mindless of her gushing pinky oozing all over the place—before they'd found themselves dancing a mad dance in the corridor by her daughter's bedroom door.

Their fingers became interlocked before she fell on her back, and he bore over her while the knife fell by her shoulder. Her daughter opened her bedroom door suddenly, catching his attention for a moment, but luckily not her mother's, who instead drew her feet in, pressed them against the intruder's gut, and launched him—with a force she never knew she possessed—up into the air and painfully down the stairs. She then rushed her daughter into her bedroom, locked the door, and dialed 9-1-1 just as the culprit burst through the sliding glass doors that led into the backyard and sped away.

Wish found her heart thumping as she recalled the mother's account of the event. Her foe this morning had eight legs, but luckily—sans any Ratatouille-akin manipulative talents—it could neither wield sharp objects nor command a vessel by its hair strands to do its murderous bidding.

CHAPTER SEVEN

*S*o many, so many, so many, so many, so many, so many, so many, so…
Nora opened her eyes and gasped as a cold chill tickled her toes.

It was like staring through wildfire, selfish flames unhinged, yearning for the touch of the invisible currents surrounding them; to consume and be consumed by the current until they roused one another to the precipice of their existence as one, and there was nothing left to be had; nothing forgotten in the path of their brief matrimony.

Nora brushed the thick veil of Sequoia-red off her face and stared up at the ceiling as she heard the apartment door shut behind Cornelius. There he was, off to Unit Four to attack his antisocial tendencies head-on. Her head was in a tilt at the very corner of her pillow, while the pit of her right knee hung over the rim of the bathtub cushioned by a folded blanket—surely Cornelius' doing—and the toes of her left foot sat just beneath the faucet.

She sat up and pulled the shower curtains back, unprepared for the scalding shine the sun would cast over her. She squinted for a moment before turning her back to it and helping herself out of the bathtub, her pillow and blanket in tow. Just as she was about to set her pillow and blanket down on the toilet seat, she witnessed a long-leg spider creep onto it. She slowly set her pillow and blanket down into the bathtub, rapidly snatched the spider, and flipped it upside down.

So many, she thought, plucking one of its legs off as if it were the petal of a daffodil. *Not so many.* Another leg plucked. *So many.* And another. *Not so many.* And another. And on she went until the final *not so many* passed through her mind, making her frown. That was a lie. She knew for a fact that there were so many. She'd seen them herself. She saw them every day, and no matter where you looked, there was no shortage of them. No matter how much she wished it wasn't true, she knew it was all too likely that quite a few of them were no different from the way her parents were.

She tossed what remained of the once many-legged creature into the toilet and flushed.

Nora heard the door open then close as she left her room, the toilet still humming. Arriving in the living room, she could hear his incessant gasping as he sat on the floor with his back against the door.

She walked around the tall granite countertops and locked the door. She stepped into the kitchen, pulled out the drawer by the fridge and retrieved a small brown paper bag.

She blew air into the bag.

She sat on her knees and rubbed Cornelius gently on the shoulder as he gasped on and on, seemingly crying, but she knew he wasn't crying.

He looked up at her.

POP! She smashed the paper bag at point-blank.

The gasping ceased.

She bunched the paper bag into a ball and tossed it into the recycle bin. She helped him to his feet. Their eyes met, her clear green eyes appearing nearly crystalline, his big brown eyes flip-flopped between dirt brown and amber. She could barely contain herself. She seemed to almost glow when she was excited, just as one would render it an impossibility that there was a white beyond the paleness of her skin.

Cornelius knew what she wanted, but it was a tad too risky.

Nora pulled him along with her over to the corner table by the recliner. She grabbed her notepad and pen and jotted something down. Cornelius looked down and tugged on the hem of his T-shirt before centering his collar. She held the notepad up to his face.

Unit?

"No, it's only been a month. We can go longer," he said.

Nora made her puppy face at him, which to Cornelius always looked more like an owl face, which was more charming than endearing, but they worked to equal effect, so he would have to try harder.

She poked her pen at the notepad.

"Two more weeks, then I'll request a unit, but not before then. Just because we're in Berkeley doesn't mean we need to be sloppy. They've got cops here too, and he's one of them. You understand?" He rested his hands on her shoulders.

She smiled.

"I'm going to go take a shower. Thanks for that," he said, pointing at the door. "Looks like it'll be a while before she can fix me, but she's good with people like us, so I'm going to continue to trust her. The day will come when we don't need the units anymore." He smiled.

Just as Cornelius turned his back to Nora to retreat to her room for his shower, he heard paper being torn. He felt her hand clap against his back and a sharp menacing instrument—

very likely, one of her stainless-steel knitting needles—being thrust into his shoulder blade. He turned back around and faced her.

She still smiled. Nora scribbled, *unit?* once again into her notepad and held it up to his face.

He put his hand around her wrist and lowered it until the notepad no longer stood between her crystalline greens and his indecisive browns. Her smile vanished, the corners of her lips declined faster than the NASDAQ that morning, and her eyes grew watery.

"Did you break your promise and do what Dr. Heller told you not to do?" he asked. She looked down at her toes and nodded. Cornelius put his hand under her chin and lifted her face back up. "Just try not looking out the window too often next time. It doesn't help your urges, okay? Pace yourself. Nothing is going to change. They'll still be out there whether you look once, twice, or ten times," he said, wrapping his hands around her.

She wrapped her arms around him and nodded, her wrinkly forehead rubbing against his shoulder. They let go of each other and Cornelius turned.

"Would you? It's difficult to reach," he said. Nora wiped her tears away with the sleeves of her pajamas and yanked out the knitting needle. Just for luck, she held the notepad up to him again and pointed to the message with the bloody needle tip staining the page.

CHAPTER EIGHT

Mr. Nelson sat there against the wall by his neighbor's garage door, hidden within the shadow of a bush, as he watched his wife and his little boy leave home for school. *Boys shouldn't be that pretty*, he thought to himself. Mrs. Nelson couldn't keep her hands to herself, always polishing their little boy as though he were a fragile little egg. It took a few beatings before she kicked those low-cut slinky summer dresses to the curb, a few more before she stopped wearing her makeup like one of Ma's escorts, and two more before she began to walk and talk like a lady: like a loving mother. *Perhaps she's due one more*, thought Mr. Nelson, before she'd let their boy be a boy.

He looked up at the silken hue of the blue morning sky and thought about the years that had passed since Ma assigned him to head one of her many buffer cities. *But why Berkeley?* he always asked himself. No one would ever wish to head Berkeley, but then again, the consequences of loyalty couldn't always be clear. Ma had given him one of her girls to keep him warm at night, a home to nest and settle in, a shop to line his pockets with, and she'd been paying his health insurance bills all these years so that she'd be the only crook he ever owed money to.

Mr. Nelson got up and ran across the street, just as his wife and boy turned the corner. A plumber's truck pulled up and stopped in front of their brown picket fence. Four men got out of the truck as always: a driver, a passenger, and two out of the back. They wore gray uniforms from head to toe, white caps stitched with a red patch that read, 'Ma's Plumbing,' and thick brown utility belts around their waists.

They followed him in. The driver and his front-seat passenger's hands were free, while the two out of the back carried either side of a heavy six-foot-long three-foot-wide stainless-steel container into the house.

Mr. Nelson left them to do their work and went into the kitchen to pour himself a cup of coffee. The driver and his passenger moved the couch. The other two set the container down, removed the floorboards with their crowbars, and pulled out dozens of tightly packed clear bags containing blue crystals from the dark recesses now exposed. They tucked the bags into the large stainless-steel container two at a time.

Mr. Nelson took a sip of his coffee and walked over to Charles' room. The bed wasn't made. He walked over to his and his wife's room. Their bed wasn't made. He walked over to the bathroom. It was spotless, with the scent of his wife still lingering in the air.

He heard the container buckle shut and returned to the living room. They set the floorboards and couch back in place. The four men nodded at him and he to them. The driver opened the door, and they all walked out.

Mr. Nelson stood at the door and watched them return to their van like little wind-up toy soldiers, Ma's soldiers.

"Hey, Nelson!" said his neighbor from across the street.

"Hey, Mark!" He waved his hand.

"What's going on?"

"It's the pipes!"

His neighbor seemed bemused. "Fuckin' pipes, man, they've got to be burning a hole in your pocket! You got these guys coming up here every other month!"

Just as the driver was about to pull away, he looked at Mr. Nelson rather earnestly. Ma hated nosy neighbors, especially ones who kept track of things they had no business keeping track of. Mr. Nelson looked at the driver and waved him away with his mug. The van pulled away and was soon out of sight.

Mark pulled open the wooden gate and walked up to him. "Hey, Nelson, ever think these guys are bilking you? Every other month is a bit much. I know the house isn't brand new, but '98, it's not that old. Sure as hell not old enough for repairs as often as you've been needing." He patted Mr. Nelson's elbow.

Mark had only moved in about a year ago and here he was, sounding like a man who spent his days down at city hall peeping around the blueprints.

"I don't think so, Mark. Think the contractor just had his head up his ass when it came to pipes. If worst comes to worst, and in two months I've got to give those boys another call, we'll just have to shell out for a full redo instead of a patch." He smiled and patted his neighbor on the shoulder. "Cup of coffee?" He held up his mug.

"Thanks, man, maybe next time. Need to get to work." Mark sped back across the street, waving.

Mr. Nelson arrived at his shop on the corner of Alcatraz just before nine. He rolled up the gates, opened the doors, and ran into the stockroom to grab a few boxes for Jordy to stock when he got in. He polished up the place, prettied up the snacks, drinks and the cigarettes behind the counter, before the first customer of the day popped in. He nodded, he smiled, rang up a few cherry swishers, and bid the fellow farewell.

It was half-past nine, with the pace of a crawl, before the phone rang. He looked at the calendar hanging on the wall and then picked up the phone.

"Nelson's," he answered with a drag in his voice. The more uncomfortable his caller was, and he knew who it was, perhaps they'd be more hesitant to call out once a month and bother being punctual and dependable for a change.

He hung up the phone and fixed his gaze at the boxes Jordy was supposed to unpack and shelve. *Six years,* he thought. Six years and he could teach his boy the ropes and save the wages for someone who wouldn't spend their every waking hour inhaling a bong and ruminating on their eventual decline into the cold bowels of unemployment.

Mr. Nelson sprung to his feet, stretched his arms, knees and back, and got to work on the boxes.

It was two in no time, and he'd just finished reading through the paper as the sweat on his forehead dried completely.

"Nelson!" a voice bellowed through the store, sending a buzz through the hands of the tween in the back corner trying to stuff a Slim Jim or two in his jeans discreetly.

The kid stumbled to the front of the store, walking between Mr. Nelson and Boyd, before Boyd grabbed the kid by his hoodie. Mr. Nelson slapped the back of the kid's head, and Boyd yanked the Slim Jims from under his shirt.

Boyd loosened his grip, and the kid ran. "I know where your mother's at, Michelle!" shouted Boyd in a rather childish tone, before looking at Mr. Nelson and laughing. Boyd put the

Slim Jims back in place and returned to the counter. "That's the future right there, man, Lord help us," he said, looking out the door.

"How's your day going?" asked Mr. Nelson.

Boyd looked down and massaged his neck before chuckling briefly. "I don't know, man. These kids. They…" Words seemed to be rolling off his tongue, just not the way he wanted them to.

Mr. Nelson unfolded a stool behind the counter and passed it over to him.

"That's alright, man, thanks. Need to get back. Berkeley High is ramping up summer activities this year. If I leave for too long, all those kids and their bodily fluids will eventually cover every surface and mutate into shit the city wants nothing to do with." He raised his hand and caught what Mr. Nelson tossed his way.

"You're going to want to juice up before heading back in there. It's on me," said Mr. Nelson. Boyd tucked the can of Red Bull in his pocket and waved him farewell. Mr. Nelson ran to the back corner of the store, returned to the counter, peeled a Slim Jim open, and figured the paper was due for another read.

He looked up at the clock and wondered if his wife had gotten to work on time.

CHAPTER NINE

Two men exited Ashby Bart station just as the shadows of dusk began to prowl. Each of them walked with their elbow facing the sky, as a large black duffle hung by the palm of their hands and rested against their backs. They walked in short strides toward the Bart parking lot, before the man with the large U-shaped face and deep placid gaze came to a sudden stop. His nearly six-foot-tall, shorter companion, with the thick lavish locks of strawberry-blond hair—which rose into waves over his head—and the pair of Bahama-teal eyes that may have sufficed in place of a flashlight—stopped by his side.

The large fellow groaned as he looked over the slim pickings in the parking lot. He pulled his phone out of his pocket, flipped it open, dialed, and held it over his ear. The shorter fellow tilted his head toward the sky, brandishing an indifferent stare. The large fellow shut his phone and stuffed it back into his pocket.

"Huh?" said the shorter fellow, as his companion appeared to mumble something to himself.

"Let's go," said the larger fellow, and they proceeded away from the parking lot toward the stairs and exited onto Adeline Street where they paused for a moment.

The shorter fellow noted that his companion seemed somewhat in awe, or perhaps he appeared in a state stranded between awe and fear. To Ma and her senior accomplices such as the leading fellow, Mr. Dillinger, by his side, it seemed that Berkeley appeared in a much darker light in their eyes. As if, while many saw it as nothing more than the tiny cauldron of activism cradled between The City and The Town, they were aware of some ghoulish secret sleeping beneath its streets.

The walking signal lit, fear and awe left Mr. Dillinger's eyes, and they crossed the street.

"Mr. Car-piss," said Mr. Dillinger.

It's Karpis, like tarps. Karpis," said the shorter fellow, Mr. Karpis, aware his companion knew how to pronounce his name but seemed in the mood to tease dryly.

"Sorry, youngblood. Mr. Karpis, be sure to watch your steps while we're here. Step on the wrong toes and you're not finding your way out. Feel me?"

"Huh?" said Mr. Karpis.

A delightful young thing, perhaps on her walk home from an afternoon yoga class, evident by her ALO leggings and loose tank-top, caught Mr. Karpis' eyes as the fading sun draped a sultry glint over her neck and shoulders, making it quite a challenge for him to resist his wicked urges. He found himself angling toward her as she passed by his side and crossed the street. Just as he was about to follow her, Mr. Dillinger put his heavy hand on his shoulder.

"No, boy. Keep your sickness inside while we're here. We're here for the boy. We grab him, pack him up, and take him home to Ma. You get nasty, we get some heat, and Ma's going to make you and me pay when we get back. Do you understand?" asked Mr. Dillinger.

"Where are we staying tonight?" asked Mr. Karpis.

Mr. Dillinger looked around as if he simply had to spot a place and it'd be theirs. He didn't seem satisfied. "Let's take a walk," he said, and he and Mr. Karpis turned and proceeded with short strides down Emerson Street.

The faucet ran hot, and steam rose as Mr. Dillinger scrubbed and rinsed his plate off.

"Well, I might just shit myself, old man. That wasn't half bad," said Mr. Karpis, setting his plate down under his companion's elbow.

"Going to wash that?"

Mr. Karpis smiled. "Well, what with you looking like you're having a good time, figured you'd want to."

Mr. Dillinger grabbed the plate. "No restaurants, are we clear? We're in and out. The fewer people see us, the better. We keep the search between sundown and midnight."

"Hey man, it was a long trip down here, grabbing take out was just a thought, I didn't mean anything by it," said Mr. Karpis.

"Boy, please. Powell isn't that far. You're just soft, but we'll get you good with it real soon. Plus, it looks like she got enough for us for the next two, maybe three days. We'll make sure we're done by then." Mr. Dillinger shut off the faucet and set the plate down on the rack, before taking off his gloves and putting them in a black plastic bag that hung from the dishwasher handle.

Mr. Karpis hopped on the kitchen counter as the old fellow took a seat at the dining table. "Come on, man, tell me how you did it. The boys back home went on and on about this freaky thing you do, and until now, I called bullshit. How'd you do it?"

asked Mr. Karpis. "I mean, she's a freaking loner, man. No family photos, a shitty flip-phone with fewer contacts than I've got pubes, and I just waxed, man. I mean, I walk up there and slit her throat, and she'll probably rot for a month before anyone finds her. Come on, old man, what's your trick?"

Mr. Dillinger yawned as he stretched while seated and massaged his neck. "It takes time, kid. Time and a lot of mistakes. Some jail time, before you get the knack for it, and even then, maybe not. Instinct. Some got it, some don't."

He stood up. "Only thing I can tell you is, don't believe that drivel about 'picking the house with the piece of shit lawn, filthy porch, crummy windows.' That doesn't mean shit about anyone. Some people are just filthy but have plenty of friends and family checking in on them. You straight with that?"

Mr. Dillinger walked into the living room and brought his large black duffle bag into the kitchen. He set it on the table, unzipped it, and tossed a small packet at Mr. Karpis.

Caught by surprise as he pondered how dull it would be, and how long it would take to find his instincts, Mr. Karpis caught the packet between his forearm and chest. "The hell am I supposed to do with this?" he asked before a small thumb-sized plastic container bounced off his forehead.

"Dye that flame of Olympus you got on your head," said Mr. Dillinger, balking at the thought that not one dweller of the night would forget Mr. Karpis' face while they searched for Ma's boy. "And put those contact lenses on. Don't know what the hell your mama was thinking giving you those eyes."

"But—"

"Not going to ask you twice, boy."

The faucet from the second-floor bathroom shut off before Mr. Karpis descended the stairs, featuring an oak-brown head of hair and dark brown eyes. "Well, who the hell are we here for?" he asked, patting a towel over his head.

Mr. Dillinger pinned a photo to the fridge. "We're here for Ma's boy."

He squinted at the photo. "Adopted?"

"Not in the legal sense, but, yes," replied Mr. Dillinger.

"How's that work?" asked Mr. Kapris with crooked brows.

"I'm not here to explain every small matter to you, young blood. He's Ma's favorite little soldier. Her numbers man. Knows all the routes and where the money is at. Ma's boys, flesh and blood, aren't too bright up here," said Mr. Dillinger, poking at his temple. "Ma wants him to take over one of these days, and what with her dealings and her… creative problem solving, that day could be tomorrow or twenty years from now, but he's the one she wants."

"Does Ma know her boys are going to dig up their Klan costumes when she kicks the bucket? No way in hell are they going to stand for it. This guy's going to get himself killed," said Mr. Karpis.

"Not my problem. Not your problem."

CHAPTER TEN

The door swooshed open as Wish charged into her apartment, undressing in the darkness on her way to her bedroom. Her keys slid across the dining table and fell by the stub of one of the chairs. Her purse dug into the embrace of a couch pillow, while her clothes littered the living room floor and trailed her to the bedroom, where she frantically searched for the light switch.

Click! Her world was once again illuminated.

She stood in front of the mirror and examined herself in her underwear. She turned once, then twice. They were fine, despite an awkward wedgie earlier in the day. She should concern herself more with what the attendees at the gallery could see.

Her phone buzzed by the nightstand. She rushed over. The first notification was from the gallery owner. She wanted to make sure Wish would arrive no later than a quarter to eight. She replied with a thumbs-up. The second notification was from Nora and Cornelius, promising they'd get there before she did. If Nora downed enough Xanax, they certainly would. She replied with a quick *thx*, and ran over to her closet.

She opened her closet and stood between its gaping jaw. Too much to wear, too little time to wear anything.

Professional, Comfortable, a Little Bit Sexy. The title of the article Wish had read during lunch hummed in her ears.

CHAPTER ELEVEN

Cornelius sat in the waiting room ruing the shine on his forehead. He recalled leaving home content with the state of his hair, how neatly he tucked in his curls, but regret always trailed him as his day carried on and moisture began its assault. He pulled the pillow on his lap closer against his abdomen while trying to smooth out the wrinkles on his T-shirt.

He glanced at the receptionist for a moment and wondered if she knew what Dr. Heller did, the kind of people she was in the business of counseling. Perhaps the receptionist was one of them.

"Rahma, please send Cornelius in," said Dr. Heller over the intercom.

Rahma looked at Cornelius, who'd already stood up and let himself into the doctor's office.

He always wondered why he was made to wait before his appointments, and if Dr. Heller's other patients also had to wait. It was, after all, her strict policy that her patients were scheduled in such a way that they could never cross paths. You were never allowed to arrive early; you were either on time or a few minutes late. Adhering to this would guarantee Dr. Heller was alone in her office.

So, the question beckoned, why did you have to wait so long?

"Cornelius." The doctor rose from her cozy wingback, reached out and shook his hand.

He grabbed a pillow from the couch, tucked it against his abdomen, and sat down.

She was the picture of uniformity he aspired to. Always a sharp pantsuit embracing her frame. A sleek, remarkably realistic black and brown wig cupping her scalp, along with features polished in such a way you couldn't tell she had skin as prone to getting oily as his, despite its darker tone.

"Tell me, how have you and Nora been settling in? Berkeley working well for her? How's the new apartment?" Dr. Heller asked without catching a breath.

"Berkeley has always been our home, and the building we bought is shaping out just fine; the apartment is sufficient. We've settled in well, but—"

"Her urges," she said, putting her pen down. "Can't you convince her to come and see me? There's a lot more I can help her with here instead of passing messages along."

"I've tried, but she's afraid that if we handle our urges separately, she'll lose herself. She doesn't feel like she'll be able to follow your rules. When she tags along with my urges, she's usually calm enough to not get carried away. She's just afraid that if she crosses the line alone, it'll come back to haunt us. She doesn't want to put you at risk, either. She knows how many people like us rely on you," said Cornelius.

She sat back, set her notepad and pen down on the table, and webbed her fingers together. "You're here for a unit, then, aren't you?"

"Yes," he replied.

Dr. Heller looked at her desk. "Is it for you or Nora?" Her narrow gaze pointed at him as she sat forward. He hugged the pillow tighter and sunk further into the couch. Dr. Heller got up and went to her desk. She unlocked the top right-hand drawer and pulled a key out. She proceeded to the polychrome abstract painting of an infant that hung on the wall behind Cornelius and set it on the floor. She inserted her key into the safe, turned it right, entered her passcode and unlocked it.

Dr. Heller sat closely next to him on the couch, her knee touching his. He shrugged half an inch away from her. She opened the calendar she had retrieved from the safe and flipped through it until she found June. A red circle was drawn around the 10th with CH—Cornelius' initials—marked next to it.

"It's been a month, just about, but I think you can go longer."

She nearly rose, before he grabbed her wrist. Their eyes locked.

"Please," he said.

"Only if you keep the bullshit out of my office. I take it you understand that this is a place of confidence and trust. Your trust in me that the knowledge of your urges will not leave this room, and my trust in you that you will adhere to my policies so we can all continue to do what we must." He let go of her wrist and she sat back down. "So, spit it out, young man. Is this unit for your urges or Nora's?"

"Nora's."

Dr. Heller returned to the safe, circled with a red marker, July 9th, and put CH next to it. She put the calendar back in the safe, pulled a Rolodex out, scrolled through it before pulling a red card out from *B*. She locked the safe, hung the painting over it and returned to him.

"I'll make an exception this time, only because Nora seems to be on edge," said Dr. Heller, handing Cornelius the red card.

"How did you know?" he asked.

"You're bleeding," she said, nodding at his shoulder. "You're going to stain my couch."

Cornelius abruptly got up and looked at the couch. To his surprise, he hadn't stained it yet.

"No more units for you until Nora agrees to come and see me. You understand?"

He nodded and then fixed his eyes on the card and its visually abstruse font.

"Same as usual. Follow the instructions and you'll have your unit. My greetings to Nora. Now get out, I've got a patient at six."

They shook hands, and she patted him on the shoulder. "Don't lose that card."

"Never," he said then left.

CHAPTER TWELVE

Mrs. Nelson stood behind the counter with a microscopic smile as she looked out the door awaiting the first customer of the day to dare to walk in. It was, perhaps, a reasonable thought that people needed bread more than they needed diamonds. She could only polish the glass display case so many times in her first few hours before it became a futile task. Brianna, on the other end of the sales floor, failed to fight off the whispers in her head and dusted off the less precious cubic zirconia display case.

Brianna dusted the case and looked nervously at the doors every half-second, even though they would hum when a patron walked in. She looked at Mrs. Nelson, who waited without a sign of worry on her face—a face no less smooth and silken than the diamonds and pearls that looked up at it from the embrace of their cozy inlays.

Brianna's heart skipped a beat as the doors suddenly hummed. She looked up, and the hope in her eyes was smitten without mercy. A man walked in, and like all the men who dared to enter before him, he was seduced by Mrs. Nelson's gaze. Her smile came into full bloom as her eyes seized his and he found himself pulled toward her like a helpless ship bound for a mesmeric whirlpool.

She watched as Mrs. Nelson smiled, ran her hand through her hair and hooked a few thick strands behind her ears while a few fell seductively by her blushing cheeks. She nodded and smiled as the man stuttered, trying to explain why he was there and what he was looking for, as though he was afraid Mrs. Nelson would be offended that he had no intention of buying jewelry for her.

Brianna remembered taking offense with Mrs. Nelson when she was first hired. Other than the store manager, Lyla, everyone else took offense with Mrs. Nelson. She could no more carry a conversation with you than an infant could do cartwheels but should a member of the less tasteful sex walk in, she was FDR on the radio and no man, boy or man-child could be more at peace. She watched as the man tried to visualize the diamond necklace and earrings on his wife, only for Mrs. Nelson—as she often did—to offer herself as the canvas for the sparkling jewels.

Mrs. Nelson walked to the other side of the counter, turned around, swept her hair off the nape of her neck, and held it over her shoulder.

"Sorry," said the man as his thigh bumped awkwardly against her bottom while he tried with unsteady hands to secure the clasp.

Mrs. Nelson turned around, put the earrings on and held her hair over her ears.

"Think your wife will like it?" she asked giggling, swaying her shoulders left and right so he could get a good view from all angles.

The man staggered out of the store while looking back at Mrs. Nelson, waving him goodbye.

Brianna put away the cleaning supplies and joined her. "Good sale, girl! Put it up here!" She held her hand up.

Mrs. Nelson hesitated for a moment before raising her hand ever so slightly for the gentlest of high-fives.

"Ladies!" said Lyla, entering the store and startling Mrs. Nelson for a second. "Who's leading?" she asked, stopping at the counter where the man had stood a moment before. "Who's going to have their pick of the new Tiffany's catalog?"

Mrs. Nelson smiled and said nothing.

Brianna looked at her nails.

"Come on, Brie. Nelson hasn't run away with it yet." Lyla joined them behind the counter and hugged Brianna's shoulder. "You're only two sales behind, and last I checked, summer isn't over." She lifted Brianna's chin. "Alright?"

"I'll try." Brianna shimmied out of Lyla's clutch and made her way back to the cubic zirconia display. "You can take the girl out of boxing, but you can't take boxing out of the girl. As always, Nelson, you've got an open invite to my gym and my ring, girl." She winked and grinned.

Still Mrs. Nelson had an unnatural knack for selling diamonds. Even as a part-timer, she was tough competition.

"I know, Brie. You've got a winner's mindset, but it's no good for you if you get too restless between seasons of not taking the prize. Granted, Nelson and Ashley got the wins for the last two sale cycles, and I've never seen you go more than a season without a win, but you're still very much in with a chance this time around. I believe in this team," Lyla said smiling and looking at the two women.

They both nodded and gave her coy smiles.

"Okay, ladies, I'll be in my office if you need anything. Nelson, I need to have a chat with you. Please follow me."

The office door shook, and they both held their breath, afraid Brianna had heard them as Lyla pinned Mrs. Nelson against it. When it seemed unquestionable that they were in the clear, Lyla buried her face in Mrs. Nelson's neck and inhaled deeply as Mrs. Nelson stroked the auburn curls of Lyla's hair. She kissed Mrs. Nelson's neck gently before freezing for a moment, lifting her face and running over to her desk to flip the frame with the photo of her thick-browed groom and their dog on its face.

"That's better. Now, where was I?" she said, brushing her hand gently along Mrs. Nelson's thigh.

Mrs. Nelson grabbed Lyla's wrist, her hands shaking and her eyes on the brink of tears.

"Babe, what's the matter?" she asked, pulling her hand away from Mrs. Nelson's thigh and resting it on her shoulder. Mrs. Nelson tried to move her lips, but the utterance of a word seemed impossible without setting off the waterworks. "Babe, be strong. We've come this far. Share that bed with him two more nights. Then, on Sunday, me, you, and Charles are out of here. My brother already got us a place down in Wyoming." Lyla brushed the breakaway tear from Mrs. Nelson's cheek. "Get out of here early and go pick up your boy."

Mrs. Nelson smiled and nodded. Lyla pulled her in and kissed her forehead.

Mrs. Nelson sat on the spinach-green bench across the street from the school, her heart lighter than a feather and her legs spry as she waited for the bell to sound its cry. She bent over, her knees touching, and unwrinkled her floral skirt around her ankles. She sat back up, made sure her red satin waistband was properly centered, and tugged her navy cardigan tightly around her tucked white spaghetti-strap top. She checked her watch. Five minutes was all that stood between her and her little boy. She opened her purse and pondered for a moment before pulling out a One-Hundred Grand bar and took a careful bite out of it to avoid staining her fingers or undoing her carefully applied cherry lipstick.

She folded the bar wrapper, stowed the bar in her purse, and stood as the bell rang. The doors burst open, and the banshees emerged from their hive, each one louder than the next, as she looked both ways and crossed the street.

She searched left and right for Charles as the little bellowing swills surged toward her before splitting like a violent current around an immovable pillar. He emerged suddenly from the doors, hand in hand with his homeroom teacher whose cologne her nose had yet to recover from—perhaps the stench of it was why she could never remember his name.

He delivered Charles to her.

Charles held his mother's right hand with his left while Mr. Something kept hold of his right hand.

"Miss Nelson, how was work today?" he asked.

Perhaps he's trying to condition me into infidelity or polyamory, she thought.

"Slow," she said, smiling as she kneeled by Charles' side and began inspecting him.

His fingers were all manners of red, yellow, and green. What backward civilization gave little kids crayons before they'd even learned to pee in a straight line? They could no more draw within the borders than they could keep it in the bowl.

Mrs. Nelson looked up at Mr. Something, masking her grimace with a smile. She stood, put her left hand on his shoulder and brushed down to his elbow.

"Mr?"

"Smith, but you can call me Anson. I don't believe I've ever properly introduced myself. Sorry about that."

"Anson. My husband and I would love to have you over Sunday night to talk about Charles' performance in class. It's very important to us that he does well and doesn't give you trouble," she said, but Mr. Smith seemed to have drifted to his fantasies as they stood in a perfect triangle, both holding Charles as her hand rested against his elbow.

"Mr. Smith?"

"Sorry. Yes, I'd love to. What time would you like me to drop by?" he asked.

Mrs. Nelson let go of them both, pulled a notepad out of her purse and scoured for a pen before Anson gave her his.

"Sorry, is that legible?" she asked, pursing her lips.

"It's perfect. That's pretty close to Dover Park, isn't it?" he asked.

"Yes, it is. So, it won't be a problem for you?"

"Not at all." Anson stooped down by Charles and finally let go of his hand. "I guess we're going to share a weekend, buddy."

"Bye now." Mrs. Nelson took Charles' hand, and just as they were about to walk away, Anson gently reached for her wrist. She looked back at him, her heart racing.

"Sorry, Mrs. Nelson. I might need that pen later."

"Oh. Oh God, I'm so sorry." She rummaged through her purse and handed it back to him. "Well then, we'll see you Sunday."

Anson nodded and smiled as they walked away, anxious to see what kind of man had won Mrs. Nelson's heart.

As they left school and walked down the street toward Martin Luther King Jr Way, Charles sped by his mother's side as she dragged him along, somewhat absent-mindedly, her cold hands shaking in his.

CHAPTER THIRTEEN

Having spent the past hour staring at his bedroom walls under the eerie glow of the plaque-tinted floor lamps, Joseph rose off the satisfactory beige futon he had retrieved from a thrift store after his interview and opened his closet. He put on a pair of shorts and a Kool-Aid-red running hoodie. He sat on the floor, opened his roller and searched through it in the thick of his clothes, yet to unpack, until he found his mp3 player and headphones.

He went over to the living room and sat on the camp chair that he had salvaged earlier by the dumpster. He pondered the complexity of his current circumstance as the rigid frame of the camp chair began to leave its impression on him. It all felt shrouded in surrealism since he'd arrived in Berkeley. Not three days before, Ma had shared with him her wishes, that should she ever decide that she'd had enough, or someone else decided that they'd had enough of her, that he was whom she wanted to take her place; where her father once sat, and where she made sure he'd never sit again.

Curiosity overcame him as he wondered how Ma took to the news that he'd skipped town for Berkeley. Had she retreated to her theater down on sixteenth to take in *Casablanca* until it reduced her to tears yet again, or had she finally heeded the calls of her father's rage that coursed through her veins and castrated those she'd assigned to watch over him?

He heard a door thump heavily, which prompted him onto his feet and out the door for what he truly needed to clear his head—a late-night jog. He locked the door and tucked his key away. He performed knee-to-chest raises as he passed by the apartment next door, then the one nearest to the stairs. As he passed, he noticed a soft glow emanating from the bedroom and seeping through the living room window as clothes appeared to be tossed hastily left and right.

At least someone's having a good time, he thought.

He jogged about two miles, eventually reaching University and California before heading back home. He recalled how much he used to run as a kid; how much he hated it. Though, if you were faster than your bullies, you eventually became too much of a hassle, and down the food chain they'd rappel for easier prey.

Before continuing down to Alcatraz and Adeline and an inch closer to home, Joseph was seduced by the florescent lights of a charming convenience store. He took deep inhales and exhales as he entered the store.

"Hey, man," said Joseph as he pulled his hoodie off his head.

The man behind the counter smiled and nodded.

He went over to the back corner and grabbed a bottle of Vitamin Water and a Slim Jim. "Sorry, man," said Joseph, putting the goods on the counter. "Got the time?"

The man looked at his wristwatch. "Seven forty-five," he said, taking Joseph's five and giving him his change.

"Thanks, see you around." He stuck the Slim Jim in his pocket and jogged out.

He stepped outside, took a sip, and looked up at the sign that read *Nelson's*, before continuing his jog home. Alas, those evening cravings would not go unanswered with such a place so close to home—and frequent they would be, until he found himself a proper TV. He crossed the street, passed by the dental clinic, and finally arrived home.

Joseph found himself dropping his bottle as he ran up the stairs, his elegantly dressed neighbor tripping over her heels as she descended and found herself caught like a tumbling Cinderella in his arms. The corridor lights fell upon them like dazzling silk sheets. Captured in a moment of uncertainty, they both said and did nothing.

The woman in his arms stared up at him, eyes wide with embarrassment. She put her hand around his shoulder as he helped her up. Decked in a black strapless dress and a fine white shawl wrapped loosely around her shoulders, she dipped to her knees, grabbed her heels and held them by her purse.

"You okay?" he asked.

"I'm fine. Thanks for saving me from breaking—" she looked over the cold steep concrete steps, "everything, I guess." She laughed nervously and adjusted her dress, which had slanted a bit.

Joseph looked at her bare feet. "You're walking somewhere?"

She looked down at her toes. "Yeah, but don't worry, not barefoot. I'm a doomed Converse girl trying to strut in heels. Serves me right." She extended her hand to him. "Wish."

He hesitated for a moment before realizing that this was an introduction and that she had not suddenly revealed herself to be a genie, offering to grant him a wish for saving her.

"Joseph." He shook her hand, embarrassed by how damp his hand was.

Wish raced back into her apartment, put on a pair of mint Converse flats—that looked as out of place as one would expect them to with a dress outside the Teen Choice Awards—and waved at him as she ran down the stairs and off into the night.

Joseph watched Wish as she ran a block down Alcatraz toward Adeline before turning back and running, her heels bouncing by their straps, toward College Avenue.

CHAPTER FOURTEEN

Wish stood across the street from the gallery, her heart sinking into her stomach as she witnessed the thin crowd of eight that included Cornelius, Nora, and Emilia—the gallery owner who was so enthused by Wish's Facebook following—wandering around her pieces.

Nora, who'd been wearing large black shades late into the night in such a well-lit gallery, caught Wish's stare. She held her hands up high and waved them in the air at the diminutive body across the street, prompting Cornelius to turn and meet her eyes. *If I can catch them off-guard,* Wish thought, *it might prove possible for me to sprint home and barricade myself in before they pin me down and drag me into the gallery.* As nimble as gazelles, those two were.

Their eyes remained fixed on each other. Wish was terrified of running down that dark street with the pair of them chasing after her. Cornelius suddenly waved at her, and she couldn't help but wave back. She looked both ways and crossed the street.

Wish couldn't stop shaking as Emilia sat her down in her office and closed the door behind them.

"I... I..."

"Breathe," said Emilia, pouring her a cup of water.

Wish pulled her phone out of her purse, opened her Facebook page, and showed Emilia the poster she'd uploaded for her gallery opening and the many likes it had garnered from her nearly five thousand fans. She pulled up the RSVP list as she took a sip of water and held her phone up to Emilia's face.

Cornelius, Nora, and the five gallery attendees turned their heads suddenly to the podium as Wish's scream bounced off the narrow corridor walls behind it. Emilia unlocked her office door, approached Cornelius and Nora, and whispered something to them. She stayed behind as the two of them went to check on Wish.

She sat in Emilia's chair, her scarf wrapped around her now red face. The two of them towered over her. Cornelius brushed his hand along her shoulder while Nora put a Xanax down on the table and pushed the cup of water closer to her.

Wish unwrapped her face and looked up at Nora. "Does it cure stupidity?" she asked.

Nora shook her head and ran her fingers through Wish's hair.

"Emilia is a kind lady," said Cornelius, as Wish hunched over his back, her thighs cradled in his hands. "Luckily, the gallery isn't booked tomorrow, so fun can still be had. Sometimes nines look like tens to me too. Anyone could've made the same mistake."

Nora, who had been twirling in circles by their side for the past two blocks, finally stopped and staggered onto all fours. Cornelius halted.

"Is she okay?" asked Wish. "How many did she take?"

"None, actually," he said. "She rented out a yoga studio."

"She's doing yoga?!" She tapped his back and he let her off.

"No, she's… painting, I think," he said, helping Nora up.

Nora pulled her pen and notepad from her back pocket and jotted something down. She tore a page out and held it up at Wish.

The French are a compassionate people, it read.

A moment of silence descended upon them.

"Thanks for the ride, Nelly." Wish kissed Cornelius on the cheek, and as he often did when another's lips touched his flesh, he produced his customary grunt and jerked away as though he was pinched.

Wish wiped his cheek with her thumb before climbing the stairs up to her apartment. She waved at them, poking her head over the rails, and they waved back at her like scarecrows swaying in the wind.

Home sweet home, the one adage she couldn't live without, sent a warm buzz over her skin. Long days such as this demanded a warm bubble bath in the company of a cold Sprite, a bag of fun-size Twix bars and a re-watch of *Dirty Rotten Scoundrels*.

Wish dug her hand into her purse and swished it around until the grim realization finally occurred to her. Had she grabbed her keys from the counter when she went back in for her sneakers?

She pressed her head against the door, her eyes too dry to produce tears, and her spirit strained beyond resistance. She listened to her own breath for a moment before slamming her fists against the door over and over, giving into despair. This was the kind of day you feared, when mundanity took you as its betrothed for weeks, maybe even months, only for the gods to remember your name, squat and relieve themselves upon your life as they laughed at you.

She fell back against the rails and drew her knees to her chest. She heard a clicking sound and looked down the corridor at Unit Three.

"Tough night?" asked Joseph, walking over to her, and holding his hand out.

"Worse, tough day," Wish said as he helped her up.

CHAPTER FIFTEEN

As Mr. Karpis and Mr. Dillinger neared Adeline and Stanford, they turned right onto Alcatraz and continued their path down to their rendezvous with Ma's Berkeley logistics man. Mr. Karpis sulked as he trailed a few feet behind Mr. Dillinger.

Mr. Dillinger turned, and his companion halted.

"What?"

Mr. Karpis shrugged his shoulders.

"Boy, we're here for a job. You think people won't remember a white boy sulking behind a black man at"—he looked at his watch— "ten o'clock at night? Shit's not that enlightened yet, kid."

Mr. Karpis murmured.

"What?" Mr. Dillinger cupped his hand around his ear, a second away from putting his young companion in a body bag and shipping him back to Ma with a failing grade.

"It's nine forty-five, you old shit. And those were fifty bucks," he said, referring to the pair of bright-lime Sunskis Mr. Dillinger had slapped out of his hands and into a gutter a few blocks back.

Mr. Dillinger got close to Mr. Karpis. "Now, who the fuck wears that shit at this time of night? Why did we dye your hair and put contacts on you if you're going to put on those shades? Let's walk and talk, youngblood. You'll learn how Ma likes shit done."

Mr. Karpis stood by his side, and they continued down Alcatraz.

"What do you think people remember? What do you think sticks in their mind?" asked Mr. Dillinger.

Ripples crossed Mr. Karpis' forehead as he squinted into the distance while his lips kissed the cool night air. "Pass."

"How many women have you been with, boy?" asked Mr. Dillinger, suddenly.

"Huh?!"

"Women. You've pleasured one before?"

"Fuck yes, I have," replied Mr. Karpis, rolling in his lips.

Mr. Dillinger seriously doubted Mr. Karpis' ability to do anything but fulfill his own needs.

"Okay, I'll keep this simple for you. Say you've been with a hundred women. No, let me correct myself. You're no Sinatra. Let's say twenty. You with me?" asked Mr. Dillinger.

Mr. Karpis bit his tongue and nodded.

"Without batting an eye, I'd wager my Granada-Gold '70 Pontiac Grand Prix that you've never loved a woman like Sinatra loved Ava Gardner."

"Christ, old timer, give me a heads up when you're about to segway us half a century down the shaft. Now, I'm getting flashbacks of when I walked in on my grandparents mashing with my grandad wearing a Sinatra mask and my grandmother wearing a skimpy rip-off of Ava's Mogambo safari outfit."

Mr. Karpis looked like he was about to be sick.

"Jesus, young blood, I wasn't expecting you to know either of them. I was expecting several follow up questions. So, you know about Ava's infamous response to a reporter in the '50s who asked her why someone who looked like her was with a 119-pounds has-been like Sinatra?" asked Mr. Dillinger.

"Only because my grandparents' sex-life was essentially fueled by the time-capsule their home was in homage to the calendar of chaos that was the hotblooded Ava and Sinatra axis," Mr. Karpis replied holding his hand over his torso. "She said, 'Well, I'll tell you—19-pounds is cock.' By making me remember all these things I've worked so hard at forgetting, you old shit, you've guaranteed that I'll be there to take a leak on your grave when you keel over," Mr. Karpis continued with a sudden odd cackle.

"Let me tell you this, I'm 165-pounds, and you better believe that I've got a whole lot more than 19-pounds of—"

Mr. Dillinger raised his hand to shush him. Ma had warned Mr. Dillinger about his companion's urges, but it felt a light matter, one he almost relegated to an unnecessary afterthought until this very moment. Perhaps it was in his eyes as the moonlight struck them. Even with the oak brown contacts, Mr. Karpis' eyes exuded an uncontrollable urge for the flesh; an almost violent energy that summoned something akin to paternal fear that Mr. Dillinger hadn't felt in quite a while. It became a sudden grave realization to Mr. Dillinger that, on this errand for Ma, his constant presence around Mr. Karpis was as vital as the mission itself. Left to his own devices, Mr. Karpis and Berkeley would prove an unholy disastrous union.

"I'm just saying, I'm not here to love, I'm here to fu—" Mr. Karpis silenced himself as he heard Mr. Dillinger cocking his gun under his coat.

They suddenly came to a stop in front of a soft neon glow from the *Nelson's* sign that shone over Mr. Dillinger's head. "Do you remember how many blocks we've walked, youngblood?"

Mr. Karpis looked back at the stretch of blocks they'd walked. "Shit, I don't."

"No one else will remember either." Mr. Dillinger smiled as they both entered the convenience store and Mr. Karpis felt like a child manipulated.

The soft-featured, dimple-chinned proprietor nodded at them while he stood on his knees restocking some snacks by the cash register. Mr. Dillinger and Mr. Karpis stood over him and he looked up at them.

He stood. "Can I help you, gentlemen?"

"Yeah. You Nelson?" asked Mr. Dillinger.

"Yes, sure am. Anything I can do for you?"

"Well, Mr. Nelson. You see, Ma's got a hankering for *Casablanca* tonight, but she's afraid it'll make her cry again," said Mr. Dillinger.

Mr. Nelson's heart almost ejected itself from his chest before buckling back into its rhythm. He looked at the door. "Just a moment, gentlemen." He walked toward the door to close it, only for two customers to wander in from the darkness of the night to satisfy their nocturnal munchies.

Mr. Dillinger turned to look back at Mr. Karpis, only to find him loitering around the Slim Jims in the back corner while glancing at the young lady who'd walked in with the tall dark young man who strutted about like a scarecrow carried by the wind.

Mr. Karpis' heart raced and wouldn't stop. *There she is again.* Regrettably in absence of her leggings and tank, but luckily the scent of her sweat still lingered in his nose. He licked his lips and swallowed as everything began to feel dry. Their eyes met for a moment, before he looked away; those bright green gems of hers liable to burn a hole through you if you stared into them for too long.

She opened one of the fridges and looked around a bit before grabbing a Pepsi. She paused, scouted the contents of the fridge further and puzzled for a moment before putting the Pepsi back, shutting the fridge and pulling a notepad and pen from her pocket.

She scribbled something down and held it up to the fellow accompanying her.

I'm dizzy, it read.

The young man gasped suddenly as he straightened the hem of his T-shirt before patting her on the head.

She opened the fridge and grabbed the Pepsi again. She stopped for a moment by Mr. Karpis' side and seemed to notice the Slim Jims he'd slipped into his coat. She smiled and proceeded to the register.

The young woman hopped onto the tall fellows back—to Mr. Karpis' agonizing envy—and they returned to the night.

Mr. Nelson sped to lock the door and returned to the register, where Mr. Dillinger left him a photo on the counter. He picked it up. "You're looking for him?" he asked.

Mr. Dillinger nodded. "Have you seen him?" He held his hand up in the air and gestured Mr. Karpis over.

"About two hours ago. He dropped in for a snack. First time I've seen him. Was out for a run, I think. Ran back down Alcatraz toward Adeline. Probably doesn't live too far."

Mr. Dillinger grinned and felt the gods smiling down on them. *Could've been neighbors*, he thought. "You looking for help around the shop?"

"Not at the——"

Mr. Dillinger put his arm around Mr. Karpis' shoulders and pulled him forward. "Mr. Karpis here is a good young man. He's looking for work while we're in town. Ma would be glad to know we've given you a hand while we're here. He'll do it for free. What time do you open?"

Mr. Nelson hesitantly looked at his watch. "He can come in nine to five tomorrow," he said, a tremor in his voice.

"What time do you close?" asked Mr. Dillinger, snatching a bag of peanuts off the carousel on the counter and opening it up.

Mr. Nelson looked at his watch again for no other reason than to escape the large fellow's stare. "Eleven."

"He'll be in nine to eleven, then. Don't worry, the boy's strong." Mr. Dillinger slapped a buck down on the counter, smiled and left with Mr. Karpis in tow.

Look as he may, Mr. Dillinger could not find Mr. Karpis. He checked the living room, the kitchen, the bathroom, and rather desperately, beneath the couch and in the fridge, before heading up the stairs and arriving at the bedroom of the house's current occupant. The padlock hung askew from the parted hinges and the door stood ajar. He put his hand on the door and gently pushed it open.

A sharp breeze pricked his toes as he entered the room, the window standing wide open as the cheap white curtains attempted take-off. He looked at the bed where the silky gray sheets spread in discord, and pale bruised thighs poked out from beneath them.

Mr. Dillinger opened the door to the closet and watched as Mr. Karpis sat on the floor, a silky gray sheet wrapped around his back and covering his crotch as he sat at an awkward angle reading what appeared to be manga belonging to the fresh corpse in the bed.

Mr. Karpis broke out into sudden laughter, making his older companion flinch. He looked up at him, the moonlight shedding a cruel, somber tone over Mr. Dillinger's eyes. "Bit late for people your age to be up, isn't it?" he said, before feeling his newly dyed hair clutched in a fistful by Mr. Dillinger and finding himself forced onto his feet and dragged over to the bed. He shook himself free from the harsh grasp and wiped the tears from his eyes. "Christ, what's your fucking damage, man?!" Mr. Karpis rubbed his head to soothe the pain.

A moment of silence fell between them like the blade of a guillotine. He witnessed what appeared to be the ghost of a tear in Mr. Dillinger's eye as the moon lit his face. Mr. Dillinger walked past him and closed the window. "What the hell happened here?" he asked, struggling to keep quiet as he looked around and saw the wine glasses by the bed.

"We got talking," said Mr. Karpis, dropping the sheet from around his waist, grabbing his jeans from the floor and putting them on. "And, at least in my opinion, if you win them over before you screw them, it always feels better when you're pressing the pillow down on their face and getting yours. I also didn't want to disrupt your quiet evening," he said winking at Mr. Dillinger. "I don't know if Ma told you, but when my nerves get dancing, my urges come knocking, and there's nothing you can do about it. This is on you, old-timer." He put on his T-shirt.

"How you figure?"

"Well, you got me volunteering in that shithole tomorrow, and customer service isn't my forte. But I'm good now, so don't sweat it." Mr. Karpis put on his coat and stood by the door. "Well, snap, I have to be up and out in five hours," he said, holding up his phone.

Mr. Dillinger nodded and shifted his gaze to the lifeless body beneath the sheets. He pulled his phone from his pocket and sent out a text draft he'd typed up earlier.

CHAPTER SIXTEEN

It was one of those high-octane days and nervous, sweaty nights that could unsettle anyone and lead them foolishly into the hole that is the contemplation of their own existence. Wish rolled around for hours in the neither too stiff nor too comfy futon that Joseph had offered her to spend the night on while he settled to rest on the camping chair in the living room. The calming cool from her shower earlier in the night had long faded and the musky zest from Joseph's body-wash—which so nearly succeeded in putting her to sleep—dissipated into the air, harried off her body by her cold sweat.

She rolled over and stared down the hallway into the living room. She wondered how anyone could sleep in a camping chair and not wake up with a fractured spine and shattered pelvis. She unzipped the hoodie he'd lent her a quarter-way down and glanced at her body, afraid she'd leave stains.

Wish zipped the hoodie back up, got off the futon a little too loudly and tiptoed toward the living room. She peeked from behind the wall and saw Joseph sprawled on the ground with his head resting on a bag of rice. She looked at the camping chair that oozed of ego as it watched him reduced to sleeping on the floor, saluting itself for what little labor it had to endure having been born out of the factory such a cruel little backbreaker.

Out of sheer spite, she sat on the chair and watched him sleep. He slept as though he were a king sleeping on an acre of memory foam and she couldn't help but resent him just a little less than she did the chair.

Wish shuddered as Joseph opened his eyes and looked straight at her. A thousand explanations rushed through her head as she contemplated explaining why she was there.

"You too?" He stretched, yawned, and scrubbed his eyes. "Couldn't sleep on it either. Tried earlier before you got back. Don't know what that futon has been through, but it's got bad energy."

"Are you okay sleeping down there?" she asked.

He sat up. "Slept in worse places, believe me. A bag of rice is as good as any pillow out there if you need it."

"Sorry for putting you out."

He waved his hand. "Please, I'm having one of those days myself. Don't mind the company. We'll get a locksmith out here in the morning and you'll sleep in your own bed."

"I think I'm out of luck there. It's a Saturday," said Wish.

"I don't think so. There are locksmiths open on Saturdays," he assured her but noticed a measure of discomfort overcome her on the topic of calling a locksmith.

"Hey, hey, it's alright. Never mind. I might have… an alternative solution," said Joseph attempting to alleviate the odd tension that had descended into the room.

He looked at her with a somewhat hesitant, timid stare.

She swept her hand across her mouth, afraid she may have been drooling, but Joseph continued to look at her rather awkwardly. "What?"

He got up, bit his lips, looked down while scratching his head, before looking back up at her. "Are you good at keeping secrets?"

Wish hesitated for a moment. It was one of those questions that usually required one who could keep a secret to compromise either their morals, their values, their integrity or all the above. From a friend, the stakes were somehow less daunting, but from a complete stranger, it was rarely a question you'd hope to be asked. However, he was kind enough not to question her over her discomfort with calling in a locksmith, so she'd have a little more faith in him.

"If you can sleep on the floor, then I don't see why I can't keep a secret," she said with a smile.

"Great! I'll be right back." Joseph ran into his room. She could hear him unzip his luggage and rummage through it, before zipping it back up and returning to the living room. He stood before her with a look of worry about him while hiding something behind his back. Wish felt somewhat afraid as she hung in some manner of suspended reality, fearing he'd present her with his mother's head to introduce them.

"You have a surprise for me?" she asked to ease her nerves and his, while not realizing her hands had rolled up into fists.

"Sorry, this is the kind of shit a black man gets locked up just thinking about to keep those CoreCivic coffers full," said Joseph, presenting her with what seemed like a fancy leather pencil case. She shook it and heard metallic clanking. She unzipped it and understood why he was so nervous. "It isn't what you think. Mostly sentimental. Belonged to my mother, but I know how to use it."

Guilt was strewn all over his face and Wish could see that he was a good man with what may have been a tumultuous past.

Given the grave crimes of her own parents, she couldn't fathom passing the slightest judgement. She stood, handed him his mother's lock-pick kit, and patted him on the shoulder.

"I'm in. But is this a good time to do it?" she asked.

"It's about four and the trash collectors come at about five, I think. We're good to go now. If you're okay with it."

"It'll be our little secret, but we'll need to keep quiet. There's a teacher in Unit Two and he might be an early riser," she warned, smiling, and wishing everyone else in their complex were twenty-nothing and had nowhere to be till noon.

2

———◆———

THE SINNERS

CHAPTER SEVENTEEN

Mr. Dillinger awoke in the darkness with a heavy head and felt the weight of his gut protruding outwards. Everything from his waist down felt weightless as blood rushed to his head. It was a few moments before he realized his hands were bound behind his back and he had been hanging upside down a few feet off cold cement floors.

Mr. Dillinger regretted the complacency that had settled into him as years of routine where he was often the one to fear left his senses dull and his muscle mass a ghost of the past. Despite the gulf in size between him and his captor—who was of similar height and stature to Mr. Karpis—Mr. Dillinger found himself befuddled by his aggressor's speed and the weight and decisiveness of their fists. So agile were they, that he found himself stumbling foolishly as though he'd been sparring with an octopus in its natural habitat before falling at its tentacles.

He rued—should he survive this—the jokes that would be made at his expense when he and Mr. Karpis returned home to Ma. While he fancied that he still had the strength in his hands to squeeze the life out of Mr. Karpis should he threaten to tell the tale, he wasn't too keen to anger Ma by snuffing one of her newer, shinier little soldiers.

Mr. Dillinger heard the rattling sound of gates being drawn up before the lights were switched on. Soft taps echoed around what appeared to be a storage unit before his captor hunched down to stare at him through their thick black desert goggles, hiding behind a ski mask.

The Den of the Proselyte was what Ma called Berkeley. Ma ran buffer cities all over the country to move her crystals around, and no number of badges or barrels pointed in her direction could do anything more than tickle her toes. However, she feared Berkeley as the travelers of Thebes feared the Sphinx. Having known the Proselyte before she'd ever gained that moniker, Mr. Dillinger heeded Ma's warning perhaps more than anyone else, but it did him little good as his worry remained with Mr. Karpis taking liberties in such a den rather than following protocol in his absence.

The masked figure brushed their hands over his bulging abdomen as if he was a cow they were about to disembowel and process. It brought a rattling chill down his spine that he last remembered feeling when Ma's father sent him out on his first kill some forty-odd years ago.

Sweat always tasted bitter when you were afraid, and Mr. Dillinger always wondered why.

CHAPTER EIGHTEEN

Cornelius rolled onto his back and sat up in his bed as the shower curtain rings scratched against the aluminum rod in Nora's room. He felt a weight on his chest as it had been a month since he expressed his urge while Nora tagged along. It hadn't been long since the days where a week was all he could bear, but such was Dr. Heller's understanding of the urges of her clientele and the psychology of weaning them off of them. Nora's urge, however, he feared, would require Dr. Heller to discover new horizons in the management of her clientele's dark desires, as it was an urge possessing a broad spectrum of interest. What he was certain of was that if Nora tagged along for much longer, no extent of intervention from Dr. Heller could ever completely diverge him from his urge and allow him to tread the path of what constituted a normal life.

He rose out of bed, opened the door to her room, and proceeded to rinse his face while she rested her elbows over the rim of the bathtub, her green eyes seeming like emerald gems peeking out from behind hauntingly silent flames. She brushed her hair off her face and watched him. He shut the faucet off and dried himself before tossing the towel at her. She laid it over the edge of the tub, then dove back into her blankets and returned with her pen and notepad.

She wrote, then held her notepad up at him.

Are you mad at me?

Cornelius shook his head. Nora turned the page and wrote some more. He approached her, hunched by the bathtub, slowly folded her notepad shut, and put his hand over her cheek. "After tonight, you'll go see her tomorrow, won't you?" he asked.

She nodded with great hesitance.

"The first time Dr. Heller helped me with my urge… I was also afraid."

He rose to his feet and walked away before feeling her notepad ricochet off the back of his head. He turned and looked into her eyes that feared nothing, could fear nothing, and would never tremble before fiends of the world or the mind.

"Sacramento," he said, just as she thought to crawl out of the tub and grab her notepad. "We leave at six tonight."

Cornelius left her room and closed the door behind him. Nora got out of bed and sat on the toilet seat. She watched intently as a little long-leg spider crawled up the wall by her side.

Cornelius stepped off the bus at Shattuck and Center. He made his short walk toward the downtown Berkeley Bart station while dragging his collar left and right, trying to center it around his neck. It finally settled just as he was about to walk straight into a pole while crossing the street. He looked up and walked like all the normal folk around him unperturbed by their clothing shifting and wrinkling.

Nora's ceaseless contemplation since their childhood was not moot—there were, indeed, so many. Too many, even—but be that as it may, he could not fathom the scale of what would need to be done to satisfy her urge. Should Dr. Heller succeed in weaning her off her urge during her lifetime, then there would be no doubt in his mind who the one true God disguised as a mere mortal could be.

He watched his steps as he descended the stairs into the Bart station and a gust of wind charged past him. He straightened the hem of his shirt and quickly centered his collar again.

He remembered how excited Nora was the day his father brought home an encyclopedia for her. Locked up in that bathroom all those years with literacy the least of her mother's care, his father thought it wise that she should learn about the vast world around her. It was all his father could talk about at the time. How her eyes lit when they pulled her from the fire. How they nearly missed her because she blended in with the flames so well. How she stared at everyone around her out in the open as though it was unreasonable that there should be so many living, breathing, walking beings like her.

Cornelius punched in his pin code, modified the amount for a two-way ticket to Del Norte Bart station, and presto. As he walked through the fare-gate and descended the stairs to wait for the Richmond train, he pondered how Nora was doing. She was often fidgety before they got to make use of one of Dr. Heller's units, and what with the physical demands it required, popping a Xanax was out of the question.

The sound of the train raced in first, bouncing off the brick walls of the underground terminal, before a chilling gust arrived in second, and the train zipped in third.

He pulled out the red card Dr. Heller had given him. Despite having read it fifty times since, it always seemed wise to refresh yourself on who to expect and when to expect them in pursuit of the instructions to a unit. He boarded the six-car train, sat next to a poor fellow with a Picasso comb-over, wrapped a dollar bill around the red card and awaited the El Cerrito Plaza stop.

So many, so many, so many, so many, so many, so many, so many, so…

Cross-legged, meditating on the couch, Nora opened her eyes and recalled the first time Mr. Harshdinger introduced her to meditation. It had been six weeks since she transitioned from a welcome guest to a legally permanent fixture in the peculiar Harshdinger household. She'd come to terms with the cruel truth that the thirty, maybe forty creatures of flesh and bone that had been staring at the burning remains of her family home that night were an infinitesimal measure of the collective that roamed the lands.

Some *six billion* walked the Earth, according to Mr. Harshdinger. It was, to her, a foolish joke at first, but it would soon bring her to tears—until Mrs. Harshdinger flipped through the encyclopedia and pointed to that which would remind Nora to smile.

One million, it read. The population of Earth roughly twelve-thousand years ago. Mrs. Harshdinger advised her to meditate with a less daunting figure in her head; to imagine, when she closed her eyes, that no more than one million fellow humans tread the nearly one hundred ninety-seven million square miles of the Earth's surface.

Nora got off the couch and grabbed a bottle out of the fridge. She sat against the door and took a few gulps before fixing her stare at the photo of Mrs. Harshdinger in the frame by the window. She remembered thinking back then, when Mrs. Harshdinger fell ill, how many like her—pure of heart—walked around with a curse hanging over their heads, fate hating all the good they'd done. While all the Mrs. Fullspakr's, like her mother, walked around with a black heart, unaware of the halo hovering above their heads, fate showering blessings over all the suffering they'd inflicted, that they'd continue to inflict, unless they were lit with kerosene.

Nora looked at the microwave. Noon was approaching. Early was always better than late. She tossed the bottle into the recycle bin, went to the bathroom, tucked her blankets and pillow beneath the sink, and readied herself for a shower.

The train took off from El Cerrito Plaza Bart and Cornelius readied himself for one of those whom Dr. Heller referred to as a unit concierge. He'd made a switch enough times. Some switches were slower than others, while some required a modicum of discretion and swift hands. Often, however, the more people around and their proximity to him made for an uneasy transaction.

He straightened his shirt around his waist, ran his hands from his chest down to his torso, and looked at the sliding doors between the car he was in and the adjoining car too intensely for a moment before calming himself and shifting his gaze to the route map next to the sliding doors. He would rely on his periphery the best he could and wait—and try not to obsess over how wrinkly one's clothes got when sitting down and how hard it was to ignore them without a pillow to hug and hide them under.

The train was getting agonizingly close to the Del Norte Bart station, and he felt his temperature rising as his neighbor angled his knees toward him, seeming to signal that he was getting off at the next stop—which Cornelius was as well.

The door to the adjoining car slid open. A woman wearing a dark headscarf, haggard from head to toe, entered the car with a baby strapped onto her back in a shawl. In her hands, she held up a cardboard sign that introduced her to the passengers as Salwa and asked for their kindness to give what change they could afford.

Many hands remained motionless, and most eyes stared out the windows or at phones, while a dollar emerged left and a five to the right, and she finally arrived before him. Cornelius reached out to her with the dollar wrapped around the red card Dr. Heller had given him and prayed that Salwa had nimble fingers. She took the dollar off him and continued forward, leaving him dumbstruck with his empty hand. Did he screw up? Was she not the unit concierge? His heart raced. He was certain that he understood the instructions on the card correctly. He looked back at her as she edged further away, and the train stopped.

Cornelius sensed a crawling chill overcome him as he felt his fellow passenger's hand slip into his pocket while they both stood up to exit.

As people flowed out the door, he made his way to a bench and sat. His legs felt drained. The switch never happened like this. Perhaps Dr. Heller was trying a new method to help him resist his urge? If he was too anxious during the switch—and she knew how anxious he became among his fellow man in small spaces—then maybe the gap between his urges would widen if the switches became unpredictable.

What terrified him most about Nora seeking Dr. Heller's assistance with her urge was how she'd handle the switches and what she'd do when the doctor experimented with her methods. Malleable could not be found in the index if one wrote a book titled *Nora Fullspakr of Little Fear.*

Cornelius would hate to watch Dr. Heller reduced to a subject of Nora's urge.

He dug his hand into his pocket and pulled out the envelope. He opened it slightly at the corner and pulled out a key and two small pieces of paper, each with an address.

Nora stood there in paralysis, the clock ticking as she seemed incapable of reaching for the doorknob, with the only certainty in her mind being that fear was not the culprit of her malaise. It was not fear—it could never be fear, not for her—but still, the beat of her heart was like a dizzy hornet falling steadily to its demise after being thwacked by a newspaper. Cornelius expected her to be ready to go once he'd returned home with instructions to the unit. It was a particular type of person who Cornelius could be enraged by, but she was not such a person. She could never anger him. However, giving him cause for concern was something she did often.

It was fate that she saw that man in the convenience store, she determined. The powers that be were telling her she didn't need Dr. Heller's help to satisfy her urge; to become another of her lambs, coming to her for a unit.

Nora reached closer to the doorknob but could not yet compel herself to grab it. She heard a sudden loud click and raced away from the door as quietly as she could and fell onto the couch. After hearing a door swing shut and footsteps in the hallway grow distant, she felt fooled by the powers that be, toying with her emotions.

She stood up from the couch, her heart as silent as dawn, before the unnecessary awoke from their sleep to pollute the world with their noise. This was not fear, it could never be fear, not for her. She reached for the doorknob and left to decide her destiny.

Her urge was hers and hers alone, and no one would dictate when and how often she could satisfy it.

CHAPTER NINETEEN

Charles looked up as the doorbell rang. His mother's long, flowy teal skirt brushed against his cheek as she rushed to open the door.

A lady stepped in hastily and his mother shut the door. The stranger was about as tall as his father. He noticed her thick black curls falling over her ears in rich layers; her nose was as cute and round as his mother's while her lips were fuller and darker, and her skin a doughy beige tone. She looked at his mother through smoldering brown eyes consumed by passion; a passion different to his father's, less brutish, and perhaps it'd leave fewer bruises, he hoped.

Charles looked back at his coloring book just as the two of them remembered he was in the room and directed their attention to him. His mother hunched by his side, ran her hand through his hair a few times, before kissing him on the forehead and returning to her room. The stranger sat on the floor across from him by the foot of the dining table, cradled his chin in the palm of her hand like an apple, and brushed her thumb across his cheek.

"Hey, sweet boy." She released his face and allowed him to soak in the magical gray and white of her pantsuit. "Do you know who I am? Did mommy tell you I was coming by today to babysit?" He shook his head. "Lyla, can you say Lyla? Of course, you can. You're a big boy, aren't you?"

Charles whispered her name.

"No, no, baby. Not Layla. *Lyla*. Like lie. Ly… la." She looked over at his coloring book. "Look at you, coloring between—"

The bedroom door opened, and Lyla looked up; his mother did not appear.

"I'll be back, baby," she said, gliding to the room and shutting the door.

Mrs. Nelson sat at her dresser, her phone and compact side by side. Lyla looked down at the doorknob and hated the absence of a lock. Self-restraint was a great feat in the presence of such beauty and its ability to play tricks with the light like no other.

She approached the dresser, stooped onto her knees, and wrapped her hands around Mrs. Nelson's waist, then pressed her forehead against her back. Their life in Cheyenne felt out of reach, even though only a few days stood between them and it.

It was the sacrifices Mrs. Nelson had to make between now and then that created the sensation it was a bridge too far. To see the Wyoming dawn caress Mrs. Nelson's face, her neck, her silken back that only Athena could've woven; she would give anything to close her eyes and wake up to that tomorrow, but of course, as history often told such tales, such beauty could not be freed without first evoking a sea of blood.

Lyla's hands slipped from around her waist as Mrs. Nelson stood up from the dresser and sat on the bed. She joined her. They fell back against the soft sheets. Lyla turned over, threw her leg over Mrs. Nelson's knee, sheltered her face in the warmth of her neck, and rested the palm of her hand over her stomach.

"Did you call?"

Mrs. Nelson nodded.

"Did they give you his address?"

Mrs. Nelson nodded.

"You sure you're up for this?"

Mrs. Nelson didn't nod, but Lyla could see a hint of a smile. "I've done worse before for Ma. I still do. But this is different. This is for us." She reached across her body and brushed her hand over Lyla's cheek.

They rose from the bed, approached the door, and just as Mrs. Nelson reached to open it, Lyla grabbed her wrist. "Maybe you don't have to. He might do what needs to be done when it comes down to it." Lyla looked at her with desperate clouds of hope darkening the creases beneath her eyes.

Mrs. Nelson smiled and shook her head. "I'm only a fantasy to him right now. He sees me, and he resents me because what he wants from me and what is real will never share the same space. Unfair resentment, yes, but he'll freeze because of it. He'll doubt himself. There won't be any real conviction in his actions because I'm not his. I'm not real to him. It can't be a fantasy; he must believe, even falsely, that there is an *us*, before he'll play the part we need him to play. Ma crosses every line she sees, and I've crossed many lines for her. This time I cross a line for us but I need to reinforce my intentions to give us a fighting chance, so I need to make sure that man believes it's a line worth crossing for him as well." She lifted Lyla's slumped chin. "Then, it's just us after this is all done."

The door shut and clicked with the turn of the key.

Lyla smiled at Charles as he looked up at her.

Be it GQ and its many square jaws or a clammy politician caught in Ma's crosshairs, all would be condemned to the past. All risen above, so long as it would soon be her embrace alone that Mrs. Nelson would sleep in through the night, and only her lips that would taste Mrs. Nelson's.

CHAPTER TWENTY

Anson sat in his father's office, hunched over on the couch by the desk. The curtains were drawn, but they were thin, so the bright flashes from the studio constantly pulsed through them and cast the shadow of his pencil onto the white-ruled pages of his notebook.

Anson hated algebra, while his father's unrelenting loyalty to disco beats and his apathy for the new wave of 90s pop, provided little encouragement in his son's quest to solve for X. Less helpful, was the hundred-square foot office half consumed by a large rosewood desk with too many dried white streaks to count, lit by a glum banker's lamp bargaining for its life.

Anson paused for a moment, confused by how his X and Y wound up on the same side, when suddenly he dropped his notebook and jumped with both feet onto the couch as the office door burst open. His father stumbled in, back first, straddled by one of his models. She was dressed, but only from the waist down, though not for long. His father stood up, still mounted, the model's chest against his face, while Anson remained the phantom in the room. They passed by him. His father dropped the model down on his desk, pulled down his pants, and flipped her over.

Anson lifted his face from the sink, brushed his hair away with his fingers, and reached for his towel. He patted his face, hung the towel, and relished the zest provided by his new face wash. He took a few steps away from the mirror and took a minute to admire how little he resembled his old man and wondered if his father's STDs had followed him into the afterlife. How wonderful that would be if only he could know for sure.

He stopped himself from grabbing his robe. He turned around and flexed his buttocks, his arms and admired the muscles of his back. He turned around and appreciated, a little too much, his full protruding chest, broad shoulders, and lean torso. He relaxed it all and returned closer to the mirror. He thought about how well they would look together. He looked down at the sink, a strand of his hair by the drain, then looked back up to the mirror. He wondered what the man looked like. The one who had won Mrs. Nelson's heart and shackled her to his name.

Anson was enthused about Sunday's visit, but he was also gripped by loud insecurities. You could tell if someone lived a happy life or a miserable one, but those indifferent, intoxicating cerulean stars she called her eyes gave nothing away—the exception, her utter devotion to her son. There was always the faint hope he granted himself. That it could still be one of these days—the two of them in each other's arms. However, to walk into a loving home tomorrow, where Mrs. Nelson had the undying love of a good man, that might just kill him.

Anson closed the windows and let the goodness of the coffee beans from the coffee machine spread throughout his apartment like java incense. He sat at the kitchen table and inhaled his coffee before he took a sip and opened his laptop.

He stared at the screen, unimpressed.

A curse—an utter curse, she was—from the moment he laid eyes on her.

Anson's stare remained fixed on the lewd images on his laptop for a few moments longer before he closed the browser and shut the computer off. He resented himself for feeling this way; she could not be blamed for making him feel the way he did, by looking the way she did, rendering any other woman he laid his eyes upon uninspiring.

He took another sip of his coffee, set the cup down, and closed his eyes.

What was it like? Her laughter. She must have laughed. Though, if you saw her, you couldn't imagine what it'd sound like. The thought would almost frighten you. He recalled the white floral-print skirt she wore the other day and how it fluttered as she walked toward the school, the white spaghetti-strap tank that fell so flawlessly over her chest, the red sash wrapped around her waist and the blue cardigan that rested over her shoulders. He remembered the madness that overcame him then. How he'd just wanted to—

The doorbell rang.

He opened his eyes. He got up, somewhat dizzy, and walked over to the door.

Anson looked through the peephole and felt the blood bustle away from his brain, gush through his heart, before heading south like a legion of baboons who'd caught the scent of tail.

Lyla sat on the couch flipping through a copy of the *East Bay Times* while her foot shook uncontrollably. Every other minute, she looked at the door, terrified that Mr. Nelson would return home suddenly, despite being reassured by Mrs. Nelson he'd be away till nine in the evening.

Charles looked up at her.

She smiled. "Hungry?"

He nodded.

She put the paper down, left the dining table, and checked the fridge for the lasagna Mrs. Nelson had prepared.

It could've been luck, but Mrs. Nelson had chosen to believe that it was the mysterious soul of the world accepting her path to freedom, despite the sticky and gruesome hurdles still ahead of her. She'd never admired Ma, nor the things she had to do for her, but for all their murk and poor dignity, those things she did made what she was about to do a less trying circumstance—at least this portion of her scheme, that is. What remained further ahead of her, she still couldn't stomach.

It surprised her that their residences were within such proximity. Ten blocks down Shattuck and left onto a lengthy block down Alcatraz and she was there. She did not expect the resistance she received when she called for his address, but perhaps the fluency with which she had to spin lies in the service of satisfying Ma's clients stood to her advantage. Who knew teachers were so well protected by their school administrators?

Mrs. Nelson walked past a few dumpsters and within a few feet, she'd finally arrived. *The Dover*, it read—the tall narrow green grate that stood between either side of the single-level apartment complex with tall stairs. She wrapped her hand across her body and over her elbow. It'd been years since they first arrived in Berkeley and no man other than her husband had touched her since. She wondered if it'd all just come back to her or if the many years of adhering to her husband's strict, rote, sexual habits had dulled her abilities to take a man to the precipice of ecstasy and back. She let out a hushed snort and a laugh. There wasn't a chance in hell that they'd dulled.

She walked up the stairs on the side of the green grate that read *1898* and passed the first apartment before stopping at the second. She brushed her hand against the door and let it rest against its cold exterior. Just as her hand drifted to ring the bell, she pulled it away and quickly retrieved her compact from her purse. After checking herself, she put it away and rang the bell.

She felt as though her chest had been filled with helium and she was ready to float away. Caught somewhere between fear and joy, she contemplated her choices before the door opened.

They stood across from one another, neither remembering what language they'd been raised to speak. Anson seemed captured in a similar realm to her own—between shivering like a naked cat caught in a cold gust or jumping for joy like a drunkard who'd just scored the Mega Millions.

Mrs. Nelson took a few steps closer to him until she stood beneath the frame of the door. It changed at that moment—the realm of emotions either of them occupied. Utterly terrified was the look on his face, while utter joy was what she felt inside as she stepped into his apartment and slowly swung the door shut as he retreated.

She continued walking toward him and he kept with his slow retreat, seemingly questioning if this was really happening—if she was truly there—too afraid to reach out and touch her and risk losing it all and waking up.

Anson's state of silent fret reminded Mrs. Nelson of her favorite type of client—the unsure and the wary. Unlike the unhinged, the manic, and the morally depraved who operated like thoughtless battering-rams, these few souls were no less taken by passion, but you could play them like a fiddle and get something out of it for yourself, too.

Anson's back finally hit the wall by the bathroom and could retreat no more without looking utterly foolish. Mrs. Nelson stepped in closer to him until the tips of her toes touched his. She raised her hand and pressed it softly against his chest. She missed the days when Mr. Nelson still had a firm figure, which had by no means entirely dissipated, but long gone were the days of his youth where calories were burned chasing down people for Ma and climbing over all manners of walls and fences. Unboxing Gatorade and Kettle chips certainly did little for self-maintenance.

Mrs. Nelson raised her left hand while her right remained over his chest and ran her fingers through his hair. His chest began to puff as his heart raced and he struggled to breathe with any rhythm. She slid her right hand slowly across his chest and over his left shoulder, and her left hand down his neck and over his right shoulder. She shook her heels off, stepped in even closer onto his feet until her chest touched his.

She smiled, held his gaze, and noticed the glisten of his forehead. She brought her lips in closer and kissed the pit of his neck once, waited, then wondered how it was that he hadn't torn anything off her yet, before kissing him again and realizing what she hoped hadn't been true. He was certainly not morally depraved—they'd be done by now if he was. Nor was he unsure or wary—they would have been at least halfway done by now. He simply and regrettably loved her or thought he did.

She stepped off his feet and walked away, taking her tank off and leaving him a trail of her clothes to follow to his bedroom.

CHAPTER TWENTY-ONE

Rahma sat at her desk, her periphery on the fellow waiting for Dr. Heller to call him in, while she scrolled through the unit database, reviewing which had been logged clean and which awaited cleaning. She looked over to the phone where line one remained blinking. She looked away to the red-eyed fellow, his hair battling between brown and gray, his nose pink and irritated, as he flipped through the paper with little interest.

Line one stopped blinking.

"Mr. McClure, the doctor is ready for you." She waved him in.

He nodded, put the paper down, winced as he stood up and slowly entered the office with his hand over his ribs.

Dr. Heller sat in her chair silently, waiting for him to drag himself over and sit on the couch across from her. A little too buzzed and seemingly enduring enough pain for nothing to matter, Mr. McClure sat down and said nothing.

She looked at him, her lips and eyes pinched. She inhaled and exhaled deeply. "Mr. McClure, as you know, I abhor inconvenience to my schedule. I am expecting someone soon, so this unfortunate meeting will have to conclude swiftly. Will you explain to me why you didn't follow protocol?" She fixed her eyes on him, despite his unwillingness to meet them.

He looked up at her, seeming intent on responding, but his lips quivered, and tears swelled in his eyes. He looked down. "My baby," he sobbed, pinching his nose between his fingers.

In a quick flash, Dr. Heller launched something at his head that concluded in a shattering sound behind him. Mr. McClure looked over his shoulder as coffee trickled down the wall behind him and the remains of Dr. Heller's coffee mug scattered over the carpet. He looked back at her like a terrified child at the dentist's office—the kind the CIA employed for less reparative dentistry.

"With all due respect, Mr. McClure, fuck your baby." She stood up and walked away to her desk. "You know what I expect from you. From all you sick fucks when you use my units. I know what you're going through and I'm telling you I can fix you, but there isn't a cure if you aren't going to follow the rules."

Dr. Heller opened one of her drawers, pulled out an envelope, returned to her chair, and tossed the envelope at him. He flinched while trying to unseal the envelope as she shouted for Rahma, who appeared speedily at the door. "Dear, would you please clean up the mess before it starts to smell? There was milk in that."

Rahma nodded while Mr. McClure flipped through the photos he pulled from the envelope. She left the office and returned momentarily with a bucket and some cleaning supplies. She stooped behind the couch and started cleaning.

Mr. McClure breathed laboriously as he flipped through the photos.

"You see the problem I'm seeing?" Dr. Heller asked. "All that shit and grime you left behind. Bitch was still hanging there with a fucking machete in her back. My cleaner tells me she was still blinking. Had to put her out of her misery."

His hands shook as he set the photos down on the table.

"You know the deal. I lend you a unit and give you the bad apple. You string them up, drain them, skin them, then kill them—whatever helps you sleep at night. But when you're done, you clean that shit up, pack it up, and my people come in for the collection, disposal and deep clean. They're not supposed to clean all of your mess. This isn't the fucking Marriott!"

Dr. Heller hunched over. "Mr. McClure," she said in a more forgiving tone. "You've been doing well. Six months since you last asked for a unit. Halfway there type of progress. Then this. What happened?"

"My baby…" He seemed unable to speak without sobbing uncontrollably.

"I know the deal, Mr. McClure. Your baby hung herself, but it's been five years. You know what I told you. Those kids pushed her, tormented her, trolled her, embarrassed her every chance they got, and she fought, but no one stepped in, it took its toll, and she couldn't take it anymore. I told you already, you can't do anything to those kids. Too close to home, too much heat. But I'll serve you all the little shits out there who love nothing more than to push kids like your daughter around. You've been good all these years, but two days ago, you fucked up. And yesterday, you took a shit all over our contract."

Dr. Heller grabbed the day's *East Bay Times* from her side and tossed it on the table. *Heroic Mother Fights Off Violent Home Invader*, the front page read with the picture of a woman wrapped in a blanket while holding her hand up in a fist minus a pinky.

"I'll ask you one last time, what happened?"

"My baby…" He winced and stood, just as a look of rage overcame the doctor. "My wife, she died giving birth two weeks ago, and the baby just—"

Mr. McClure found himself confused for the longest two seconds of his life. He watched as his hands shook, while in his periphery he could see the tip of Dr. Heller's pointed heels. Everything was slanted, and he watched as his body fell to its knees and tumbled away from his field of vision in a spasm. The last thing he'd ever see were the soles of his own shoes and Rahma standing behind the couch with a long, glimmering, curved scimitar in her hands.

Dr. Heller looked down at his head, then looked back up at Rahma. "Sorry, dear, I know you prefer firearms, what with your father's former occupation, but this idiot was getting on my last nerve. Call in the crew for a deep clean and check on Kyle. See if he's picked up your gun yet."

"What about your one o'clock?" Rahma held the scimitar down by her side, stained with Mr. McClure.

Dr. Heller turned her head to the door. "You fine with this, Mr. Dillinger?"

Rahma gasped and dropped the scimitar on the carpet. She hadn't noticed the hulking frame of the man leaning on the other side of the door frame.

The large fellow shrugged indifferently, entered the room and turned his large, droopy gaze over Rahma.

Dr. Heller and Mr. Dillinger sat in the waiting room, the office closed for the day, as Rahma returned to her desk, pretending she couldn't hear their conversation.

"Is your crew quick?" asked Mr. Dillinger.

"They better be. They know our line of work doesn't tolerate delays. How is she? Is my sister still spreading that stuff about me? Still telling people, 'Beware of the Proselyte?'"

"Well, in her defense, you're running some pretty nasty shit down here. No one knows who you've chewed up and who you've got in your pocket."

"So, I assume she's not coming down here to see me anytime soon? Holding up in front of the screen, as usual, I guess?" Dr. Heller looked up at his large face and droopy eyes, remembering the days he used to drive her and her sister to school before anyone knew them as Ma and the Proselyte.

"Did you get my message?" asked Mr. Dillinger.

She nodded.

"And?"

"I can't help you. I know my sister well, even if we haven't seen each other all these years. The ones she calls Karpis she sees potential in, but they tend to be a handful in the beginning. However, if they turn out the way she wants them to, then she may just call them Dillinger one day. You've been around longer than the two of us. Dillinger and Karpis weren't a thing back when our old man ran the business, but you know she's much smarter than he ever was. Our father was fine with his thumb on The Town, but she always had more grand ambitions. An eye for 'meaningful cataclysms' as she once told me. Leave him be. If he gets out of hand in my home, I'll put your boy down."

Dr. Heller stood and put her hand on Mr. Dillinger's shoulder, brushed it over his cheek with a glint of the past in her eyes, and left the office.

He sat there for a moment, then directed his gaze at Rahma. "You're looking healthy, young lady. Seems like you're getting your sleep."

Rahma looked at him bemused.

"He's on to number six since you dissolved your partnership with him, you know. Ma can't seem to find him a partner who'll last. A week or two in, and insomnia causes them to lose their minds. Number six looks promising, though. We'll see how long she lasts." He smiled.

She remained silent while holding his gaze.

He stood up, approached the desk, pulled a photo from his pocket, and held it up to her. "You've seen our boy?"

Rahma examined the photo of the young man. She shook her head.

Mr. Dillinger grunted.

"Well then, I'll see you around. Got things to do. Ma sends her greetings. She says you and Salwa are welcome back any time." He put the photo away and left down the stairs.

She looked back at the monitor, quickly ignoring her past with that man and focused on more important things. So many units, so many deviants, so many cleaners, and so much information. She wondered how much longer Dr. Heller could maintain all of it.

Rahma could still feel the scimitar in her hand and wondered if her father had felt that same phantom blade in his hands all those years he spent as an executioner for the Kingdom in the desert.

CHAPTER TWENTY-TWO

Wish would often suffer a recurring nightmare whenever she'd been working on a piece to add to her portfolio, and loathe she did those sweaty nights where she'd dream of herself in a gallery waiting to deliver her speech. The one describing her inspiration that would require her to delve into her childhood like every other penniless artist. She'd step onto the podium, smile at the crowd—surprised by the great turnout—and as she would reach into her pocket for her notes, her hand would meet her damp, slippery thigh and she would try again and again, afraid to look down, before relenting, looking down and witnessing her utter nakedness as lights shone upon her from the ceiling, revealing her every flaw.

This was *worse*.

What she felt right now, her cozy mint and pink toned, paisley print duvet pulled over her breasts as the scent of dry sweat crawled up her nose was much worse. Joseph flipped through her portfolio, the sheets hanging just over his abdomen as his left leg poked from beneath the covers and his head rested against the headboard.

It's okay, she assured herself. It was a reasonable progression of events that had led her here. First, the standoff with the eight-legged horror show. Second, playing Find the

Finger in a home which so nearly hosted Find the Body. Third, falling into the strong arms of your new neighbor just as fate had intended to shatter every bone in your body to spare you from the embarrassment of your Facebook faux pas, and perhaps gain you sympathy on the following night. Fourth, attending your first gallery opening the day before anyone would care to show up because nine and ten somehow looked too much alike when you sent out the invitations. And finally, taking refuge in your new neighbor's pity and granting him the privilege of picking your lock. Then, for no reason other than the need to overwrite those horrible memories, pin him down, mount him like a stallion and ride the carousel like the lever is broken, until the line between yesterday and today turned into one giant delightful blur.

"Huh?" Joseph flipped the page and looked at her as she seemed to whisper something.

"I need to use the bathroom," said Wish.

He wondered what the significance of the message was as they were in her apartment and the bathroom was right out the bedroom door. "Oh. Okay?" He turned his head slowly back to her portfolio.

"Please close your eyes."

"Oh, yeah. Sorry, sure." Joseph set the binder down on the bed and put his hands over his eyes, feeling silly.

"I'm not crazy, I swear," said Wish, slipping out of bed. "I know we've seen plenty of each other, but still, it's like the one between the sheets and the one the morning after are two different people. For me at least." Her voice grew distant as she shut the bathroom door behind her.

He smiled, put his hands down and picked the binder back up, then shuddered and dropped it.

"DO YOU HAVE HEADPHONES ON YOU?" Her voice shook the bathroom door and probably her neighbor's door.

The bathroom door swung open, and Wish emerged in the comfy embrace of a blue tank and her heather gray pajama sweats.

"You don't have to leave," she said, as Joseph seemed to have gotten fully dressed.

"Quick run over to the convenience store. Feeling some Gatorade. Want anything?"

She looked up at the ceiling, their dance in the dark flashing before her eyes for a moment.

He noticed she'd spaced out and her cheeks grew flush with color.

She looked away from the dangerous slate of the ceiling reflecting their summer fever and over to him. "Sorry. No Gatorade for me, thanks."

Joseph left.

Wish returned to her bed, picked up her binder, looked through the pages and wondered what he'd thought of her work. Her fingers tightened around her binder as a sudden thump shook the wall behind the bed. She looked up at the wall as one does, even though they can't see through it.

It was quiet for a moment. Then it began. The unison of pleasure. Two choosing the wild dance in the light, their voices ebbing and gushing forth in perfect harmony. *Sounds like Anson's having a bit of morning delight.*

Wish dropped her binder and buried her face in her pillow, dreading the turbulent awakening Anson must've suffered as she and Joseph romped through the early hours of the morning like horny, lubricant-starved Transformers.

CHAPTER TWENTY-THREE

Jordy sat on the stool and rested his elbows on the counter as he looked over at Mr. Karpis—or Alvin, as he had been introduced to him—on his knees restocking the Dasani. He looked over to the back of the store and at the door to Mr. Nelson's office. It didn't matter what you had going on, if you called out one day, he'd expect you in the next, whether you had finals, suddenly contracted Hepatitis C or were expected to brief POTUS.

Jordy looked at the store entrance, and with no one in sight—people did have better things to do on a Saturday—he walked over to the other side of the counter with a duster and ran it with little motivation over the shelves. Perhaps the masses were still reeling from the exit of the Stars and Stripes at the hands of Ghana, and either remained in bed, rolled down to the Marina to soak in some rays, or—still on a high—remained fixated to their TVs until the kickoff for bronze.

Mr. Karpis looked over to his right as Jordy drew closer.

"Hey man, how's it going so far? Thrilling, isn't it?" He grinned, unsure what it was about Alvin that made him feel somewhat wary. Perhaps it was owing to his rather unnatural look. His oak-brown hair and eyes outshone and out of place in the presence of his pale skin and blond eyebrows and lashes.

"It's cool, man. Dealt with tougher things." Mr. Karpis looked over, nodded, then stood and shut the fridge door. He shifted over to the neighboring fridge, pulled a few boxes along with him, and started from the top.

Jordy took a few steps back and made way for him. "You ever work at a convenience store before?"

Mr. Karpis shook his head while stocking away.

Jordy looked over at the entrance. Still not a person in sight.

"Worked adjacent to a convenience store," whispered Mr. Karpis to himself, unaware of his colleague's keen ears.

"Adjacent? What do you mean?" Jordy looked back at him.

"Kept my eyes on the produce at night. Made sure they didn't get mishandled or damaged."

"You mean like deliveries? You worked in receiving?"

Mr. Karpis turned and looked at Jordy, pondering what other words besides *produce* he could use to substitute for Ma's ladies of the night. Their eyes froze over one another's before steps emerged into the store and they were in the company of another.

Mr. Nelson sat back in his chair, held the phone over his ear, and listened. It took a great effort from him to take in all that Ma was saying while trying not to worry too much about what conversations Mr. Karpis and Jordy could be having out there.

Ma was not one to be asked to repeat herself.

"I don't think he will be an issue," he replied to her question about his nosey neighbor; news traveled quickly back to Ma.

"He is—"

"No, I can't guarantee that."

"He's got a young boy. Sees him on the weekends."

Mr. Nelson felt overcome by a sudden wave of heat. He unbuttoned his collar, grabbed his handkerchief, and wiped his forehead. "Maybe we can change the schedule."

He held the phone away before Ma's scream could tear a hole through his eardrum. He held the phone close again. Ma alternated between hot and cold very quickly and with little warning, and it often took the novice a few bleeding ears before they'd become attuned to her temperament. "I understand. Sorry, Ma."

"No, I'm not hiding anything."

"He's healthy and doing fine. His mother took him to school today."

"No, not stupid. His mother just likes him to get a foot ahead of the other kids running around and watching TV all summer."

"She's fine."

"I've been setting her straight. She's almost got a proper dignity about her now."

Mr. Nelson popped another button loose, grabbed his handkerchief and wiped his forehead again. "No, I'm not—"

Ma asked him to wait for a moment. He could hear a muffled voice in the background. It didn't matter who it was, whether you could make out the words or not, pleading always sounded the same. Perhaps a few of Ma's crystals went missing. Perhaps someone spoke to a pig without realizing it was one of Ma's pigs. Or perhaps Ma had invited a date back to her theater to enjoy a screening of *To Have and Have Not, Sabrina,* or—if Mr. Nelson knew Ma as well as he thought he did—*Casablanca*, and the poor fellow, taken by her charm and seeming vulnerability, pulled out his phone without realizing the creature she often turned into when one disrespected the silver screen like that.

He listened as Ma's boys powered up the baler, at which point, the muffled pleading turned into loud shouting, and it became clear that hypothesis number three was the truest of them all, as he could hear the fellow yelling out, "Babe!" He held the phone away from his ear as the man was likely bound and tossed into the baler. The following screams of agony were impossible to explain.

Ma held her phone back up and apologized for the abrupt halt to their conversation. She asked him again.

"Can't say for sure, but Mark may have checked out the blueprints."

Mr. Nelson rested his elbow on his desk and pressed his forehead against the palm of his hand. "A weekday would be best. His boy stays over on the weekends."

"He's ten, Ma."

Mr. Nelson dreaded that if Ma ever found out that Mark's son was eighteen, he just might find himself in that baler one of these days. "I'll drive us up to the cabin on Wed—"

"Tuesday, then. We'll head up on Tuesday and return on Thursday."

"I will. We miss you too."

Mr. Nelson hung up the phone, stood, buttoned up his shirt, wiped his forehead one last time and went to check on Mr. Karpis and Jordy.

CHAPTER TWENTY-FOUR

Nora sat on the bus stop bench, defeated from her day's search, and thought to return home and tell Cornelius she'd gone out for a walk. She'd only seen the man once last night. She hadn't the slightest idea who he was, what he did or where he lived, but her maddening desire to satisfy her urge alone without forcing Cornelius to share his led her down a path of delusion. The Slim Jim thief was more in the mold of those who triggered Cornelius urge, but then again, anyone and everyone triggered her urge, so he'd do. Tonight, would mark the first night they'd satisfy their urges separately, if she had her way.

Nora contemplated her next move. Since meeting his eyes last night, she couldn't shake the Slim Jim thief from her mind. The question remained, where could she find him?

She reached for her thigh and pinched herself. The thought itself was a sin, but the fact remained, if you knew the very dark underbelly of Berkeley like very few did, the Proselyte was the one with the keys to all the doors. To go to her, however, would be to slide under her thumb as many did, Cornelius included, and have her dictate the trajectory of your urge with the end goal of eliminating it.

Nora looked across the street again and felt the invisible hand of fate brush gently against her face. There he was, suddenly.

A man wearing a red hoodie exited the convenience store she and Cornelius had briefly visited the night before, and not a minute later, the Slim Jim thief poked his head out, then tiptoed after him. Seemingly realizing he'd forgotten his apron on—perhaps he worked there—he removed it, ran back into the store, then back out, following the trail of the other fellow.

Red hoodie man had reached the third block approaching Adeline, Slim Jim thief followed a block behind, and she stood lazily—to not arouse suspicion—and proceeded forward on the opposite side of the street with her eyes on the jerky thief.

It was a few seconds before the three of them were on the same side of the street and she watched them from a distance. Slim Jim thief had stopped outside the dentist's office and red hoodie man had gone up the stairs of The Dover. She couldn't say for certain from where she stood, but he seemed to have entered Wish's apartment.

A moment later, Slim Jim thief pulled a phone from his pocket, dialed a number and had the briefest of conversations before proceeding down Alcatraz and turning left on Shattuck. After several blocks, he turned right into Emerson and entered the sixth house down the road.

Nora recalled how happy she was the night that house burned down; how her mother screamed, how her father cried and how bothered by the flames those two rats were while she swam through the red, lashing tongues. She remembered sharing one last glance with her brother as he sat up in his bed, a peppery wall standing between them before a hulking figure hauled her away like an enchanted golem.

She wondered if Slim Jim thief would scream for her. Only the night would tell.

She walked away and pulled her phone from her pocket to note the address before it buzzed in her hand with Cornelius flashing across her screen.

Cornelius' heart raced as he exited the stairs into the corridor. He turned left and proceeded down the hallway. He walked as fast as he could without appearing to run, every click, every creak liable to force him into a dash. If anyone should emerge, he would greet them. No nodding. No awkward smile. He would say hello without hesitation and brimming with confidence.

He arrived home. His heart purred like a cat as he swung the door open. He pulled the envelope from his pocket and set it down on the counter.

"I'm home! Are you ready?" He took his shoes off and fell back onto the couch.

He brushed his hands down his shirt, flattening the wrinkles before he pulled his phone from his pocket and scrolled through the news.

"Nora, you ready?"

He put his phone down, stood up, and got the envelope. He pulled the key and the two slips with the addresses out. Same game, different delivery. The blue paper took you to the car, keys under the bumper, the subject's folder in the glove compartment, and a black outfit in the trunk. The green paper took you to the storage unit, and the key in his hand opened the unit where the subject of his urge would be waiting in restraints to receive the punishment they were owed.

Cornelius recalled the long pause when Dr. Heller first asked him, *maim or kill?* He'd never thought about it up until that point. He had an extreme distaste for anyone who took anything that wasn't their own, big, or small, with complete disregard for those they harmed. The thought of them made his skin crawl. They didn't deserve to live, and while he couldn't fathom taking a life, to maim them and leave them to live with their scars fully aware their pain was a result of their sin—and he'd make sure they were aware when he was done with them—that put him to sleep like a baby wrapped in the smoothest silk swaddle. He remembered a past when he didn't feel this way, before his mother's incident. When he had negative opinions about thieves, and really anyone who intentionally harmed the people and community around them, but that was it. It was a negative opinion, not an all-consuming murderous itch. It was like some neural network overpass in his brain existed simply because his mother did, and when she no longer existed, its structural integrity disintegrated leaving only a dark plume of smoke that touched and darkened everything that once constituted his right mind.

He wondered if Dr. Heller could really do it—cure him.

He went to the bathroom and knocked on the door. "Nora!"

He opened the door after a few seconds of silence. Everything was in place but for her. He raced to his phone and dialed her. It rang and rang. He hung up.

Cornelius put his shoes on, tucked the key and the pieces of paper back into the envelope, and dialed Dr. Heller.

CHAPTER TWENTY-FIVE

Anson's head sunk in his pillow, bounced back up, and then settled gently. He gasped for air, feeling the kind of high he never realized possible, uncertain whether he'd just been kissed or choked or both as she sat on the side of his bed, grabbed her skirt from the floor and got up to gather the trail of her clothes on her way to the bathroom.

Mrs. Nelson couldn't help but find herself grinning as she made her way to the bathroom. Ma's girls often liked to close with The Stopper, as it often left their clients breathless, and they'd be spared any cringy monotonous tributes.

She stepped into the bathroom and locked the door behind her just as *woo!* ricocheted off the bedroom walls. She held her hand over her mouth and tried not to laugh. She felt silly, but it felt nice. Mr. Nelson was much like most of her former clients, albeit slightly younger, with a penchant for a sandwich afterward, and the compliment never came.

Mrs. Nelson hung her clothes and pulled the shower curtain open. L'Oréal Total Repair Five shampoo, conditioner, and damage erasing balm stared down at her. Anson had potential, regrettably. Just as she was about to step into the bathtub, she found herself stuck in time beneath a dense overcast. She looked down at the palm of her right hand facing up in front of her torso. She thought you only saw your life flash before your eyes when on the cusp of death, but could it also be triggered when you were about to cost someone else their own life? Catching herself off-guard as she began to cry, she slapped the palm of her right hand over her mouth.

Anson stood and turned to the sound of the bathroom door opening. Mrs. Nelson emerged, sped over to him, and hugged him. Anson's heart calmed as she loosened her arms around him. She stepped away from him and made her way to the door. He grabbed her wrist. She turned and saw the fear in his eyes; the fear that this would never happen again. Mrs. Nelson stepped closer into his frame, put her finger under his chin, drew him in and kissed him. She let their lips hold a few moments longer before brushing her hand over his cheek and retreating.

Just as she feared that he wouldn't let her go, his hand loosened, and she was free.

Anson's instincts were right. This would not happen again.

CHAPTER TWENTY-SIX

"Shit, honestly, I can't remember. I don't think we were that loud. Plus, anyone bothered by us last night is not thinking about us anymore," said Joseph, referring to Wish's neighbor in Unit Two while sitting in the kitchen sipping his Gatorade as she made herself a smoothie.

"So?" She looked at him. "Any thoughts?"

He felt stumped. He wasn't one for critiquing art and was too wise to critique that which belonged to the one he'd only recently joined in carnal exploration. "It's really good. Different. I think a lot of people will like it, especially people our age who grew up watching sitcoms. They'll probably make a game out of it, trying figure out what show it's from. Probably had that in mind when you started the project?"

"Not really, but it did eventually occur to me after reading a few comments on my Facebook page when I put them up the first time." Wish took a sip of her smoothie and brushed her hair over her ears as she joined him at the table. "I don't know, though. I watched those shows so much when I was young—and these days, don't even get me started—and I always found myself wondering, what are they saying? Those extras back there. At some point, I was just droning through episodes, focusing on the extras, and completely ignoring the actual plot.

Then it just sparked. I spent weeks gathering hundreds of freeze-frames of scenes, picked out my favorites and went to work. I'd—" She seemed discomforted.

"What's wrong?" Joseph asked.

"I'm blabbing, sorry."

"Come on, lay it on me."

"Well, basically, I decided to put together a collection of untitled sketches where I put all the details into the extras and left the main characters as just white outlines of themselves in the scene. Most of my followers will kind of try to just figure out the show, which honestly isn't that hard—especially with Frasier and his head—but then some will kind of get all competitive and try to nail down the season, the episode, and the few fanatics will go as far as nailing it down to the minute."

He smiled at her.

"What? It's sort of fun. Feels like they genuinely care, and for an artist, that's what matters most, that people feel engaged by your work." She got up, walked to the sink, and rinsed her cup.

"Want to scroll through your sketchbook?" he asked.

"I've scrolled through it a million times, believe me."

"Come on, one more time won't hurt." A sly grin overcame Joseph, before it vanished as he realized how cheesy what he did was, but it was too late to turn back time. *Regret*. He felt overwhelming regret.

Intrigued, Wish went into her bedroom, grabbed her sketchbook from the bed and scrolled through it. At first, all seemed unchanged. After scrolling back and forth through it, she caught the faintest of pencil strokes at the top corner of each page. She looked closely. She turned to the next page, then the next, then the next, and at the top corner of each page she found the title of the show, the season, the episode and the very minute of the scene as she thought she could only ever remember.

She turned and found Joseph standing at the door. "Sorry, I don't know why I did that." He was too embarrassed to look her in the eyes.

"You didn't have a very productive childhood, did you?" She smiled and bit her lips.

"Actually, I got lots of shit done. I just remember a lot about most things I enjoy. How about you?" he asked, looking up at her, happy she didn't find it cringy. *But she probably did.*

"I hope you don't take this as approval that you more or less vandalized my art," said Wish with a wry smile.

Her sketchbook thudded against the floor and Joseph found himself tugged into the room by his collar and dumped onto the bed before hearing the door slam shut. Joseph smiled as he looked up at her as she sat on his thighs and looked down at him.

"I skipped a few grades, so I can't say my youth was fruitless, either. I just remember a lot about most things I enjoy, too." Wish smiled as Joseph sat up, wrapped his arms just beneath her hips, and kissed her under her eye, and continued down to her lips as his hands slid up her back.

CHAPTER TWENTY-SEVEN

*F*ound *the fucker.* Mr. Karpis' words still slithered along the walls as Mr. Dillinger sat at the kitchen table flipping leisurely through the paper.

Footsteps thumped down the stairs and Mr. Karpis appeared in the kitchen clad in black before his much wiser, much-tempered companion. "Well?" Mr. Karpis said, pulling his gloves on—black as well, of course.

Mr. Dillinger continued to flip through the paper.

He huffed. "Hey, you good to go, old man?"

Mr. Dillinger directed his droopy gaze away from the paper and to his fuming accomplice. He folded up the paper and put it down. He stood, walked past the black-clad young fellow to the small window over the sink and pulled the shades back.

"Come here, boy."

Mr. Karpis joined him and looked out the window. He immediately felt the back of his neck grabbed harshly and shoved closer to the window. He tried to shake him off, but the older fellow was stronger than he seemed.

"What the fuck do you see?" Mr. Dillinger directed his heavy, disapproving gaze at his younger accomplice as his grasp grew tighter. "You ever snatch someone for Ma?"

Mr. Karpis couldn't shake his head without having his neck rung.

"No," he grunted.

"Why do you think?" He tightened his grip just a little more until his young companion's eyes turned bloodshot. "Because Ma doesn't send out thoughtless fools for a grab. You seem almost normal, so you better start thinking straight." He released Mr. Karpis' neck and returned to his paper. "Get your ass back to Nelson's. I don't know who told you you're done. Leave the address and we'll meet out there at around nine." Mr. Dillinger looked up at Mr. Karpis, wiping the tears from his eyes. "Are you about to move or am I going to have to move you?"

The door shut behind Mr. Karpis. Mr. Dillinger put the paper down, then picked up the torn upper corner of a magazine the younger fellow had written the address on.

The Dover, 1898 Alcatraz Ave, Unit 1, it read.

He walked over to the stove, turned on one of the burners and fed the address to the flames.

CHAPTER TWENTY-EIGHT

Dr. Heller put her hand over his, as she and Cornelius sat in her silver Ford Focus parked in the lot across the street from her office. Even in her hand's embrace, his hand still shook. She turned on the AC as his chest began to sweat through his shirt.

"I'll find her, don't you worry. Brought the envelope with you?" she asked. He nodded, pulled it out from his pocket, and handed it to her. "It's okay. We'll put the car away, extract the subject from the unit, store her off-site for you, and get you in that unit in a week or two." She put her hands over his shoulder.

He looked at her, the curiosity in his eyes momentarily subduing his hand's tremor. He was keen to learn about the subject waiting to suffer his urge. She smiled. "An accountant down in Fremont, can't help herself but lift bracelets from Macy's on her lunch breaks. Got about three hundred dollars' worth stuffed in the garden gnome. Small fry, I know, but I'm still working on an overpaid, under supervised, state employee who's been creatively embezzling state funds to support his annual Amesterdan excursions for half a decade now. If we can get him in the next week or two, I'll serve him up to you instead."

A thief was a thief. Never too big, never too small. They all stunk the same to Cornelius. "Does she have kids?"

"Two, but the dad can keep an eye on them until you're done with their mother." He pulled his hand slowly from under hers. "I told you, if you prefer them single, we can continue doing that. No shame in it."

Cornelius shook his head, his nose pinched in a grimace he was struggling to control. "No, they'll learn from growing up watching her suffer. When the opportunity presents itself to them, they will be clean from the predisposition their mother was consumed by."

Dr. Heller smiled.

"Store her, please." He rested his back in his seat and tried to calm himself.

"She is impatient, but she isn't a fool. Whoever she's identified as the worthy subject of her urge, Nora will be taking them to one of my units. Likely, a unit you've used before. I'll have my people keep an eye on them and let me know when and where she turns up." Dr. Heller sat back.

"What if the BPD catches her first? I don't think she's got a plan. I don't know what she plans on doing to get the body from A to B. This is a mess, sorry."

"Go home. You leave this to me. I'll call you when she's found." She reached across him and unlocked his door. He seemed a bit more at ease, but he'd probably start panicking again once he got back home.

Cornelius got out of the car, shut the door, then opened it again and poked his head in. "Why aren't you in your office?"

"A plumbing disaster. Tried cleaning it up, but it got out of hand. Got someone over taking care of it now. We'll talk in the office next time. Come on now, go home. I'll let you know once she's found."

He shut the door and made his way out of the lot and out of sight.

Cornelius locked the door behind him and slumped to the floor.

Huh, huh, huh, huh. He couldn't stop the incessant gasping.

He crawled over to one of the kitchen drawers, pulled out a paper bag, and breathed into it.

Huh, huh, huh, huh.

He caught some air in the bag, held it up to his face, and *POP!*

Huh, huh, huh.

It was as he predicted. It only worked when someone else did it.

CHAPTER TWENTY-NINE

Lyla looked up at the door fearful, as she thought she heard a squeak while brushing her fingers gently through Charles' hair, who'd fallen sound asleep with his head on her lap.

She held her breath for a moment, and once assured Mr. Nelson hadn't walked in and everything hadn't gone to hell, she breathed a sigh of relief and looked back at the TV.

She wondered if it had been done. If Mrs. Nelson had gone through with it or if she'd lingered outside his apartment before deciding to spend her afternoon at a café. It was, at least, what she hoped had happened. It was bad enough that Mr. Nelson would lie by her side one more night than he deserved, but to give herself to another man for their plan to work—the simple thought of it turned Lyla's stomach. Lyla much preferred to put one between Mr. Nelson's eyes herself and be done with him. However, Mrs. Nelson insisted that they commit to the current plan that would paint a better picture to aid their escape to their new life. Her strength was owed to the darkness of her past and present; a case of falling down a bottomless sinkhole, daunting to most, but not to those who'd fallen into such depths repeatedly in a life of traveling from tragedy to tragedy.

The door swung open.

Her heart leaped into her throat like a carp startled by a boat's motor as her fingers froze in Charles' hair. She shuffled through her mind for a story, any story, but all her concoctions dissipated as Mrs. Nelson walked in, her smile warming Lyla's heart.

CHAPTER THIRTY

Wish stood up there in her strapless black dress, her white shawl wrapped loosely around her shoulders, while holding her phone in her hand, surrounded by a half-changed supporting cast. Her followers descended upon the gallery and swarmed around her works like hopped up trivia-hounds, each aiming to prove through their answers that it was they who frittered their youth away before the mighty television.

Joseph stood tall amongst them, sampling hors d'oeuvres, and shot her a smile from across the room.

She looked down at her phone, but neither Cornelius nor Nora had responded to her texts. Her hands grew clammy as she thought about them. They were the types who'd always show up no matter the gravity of the occasion.

Emilia made her way through the crowd toward the podium.

"Are you ready, mon cher ami?" she asked, wrapping her arm around Wish's shoulders.

Wish nodded and stepped up to the mic. "Excuse me. Um, excuse me." She looked back at Emilia as the bustle of conversation continued to wrinkle the airwaves.

"People, people! My girl's up there trying to get your attention and get his party started! You in?" Joseph tried but failed to get the attention of the competitive pop culture crowd. The hors d'oeuvre he was chewing certainly didn't help him get loud enough. Failing to come to her aid, he looked at Wish standing behind the podium, embarrassed by his own continued effort to process the hors d'oeuvre in his mouth, and just wanted to disappear.

Emilia stepped up to the mic. "Excusez moi, tout le monde! Please, quiet down!" she said aloud in a commanding yet elegant tone without it turning into a harsh shout.

The crowd fell to a deathly silence and all the heads turned toward the podium.

Wish smiled, and Emilia gave her a wink and stepped back.

Wish stepped up to the microphone. "Thanks for coming. A horrifying thing happened around this time yesterday evening."

Joseph and Wish walked side by side and turned left onto College and Alcatraz. Wish thought to reach out and hold his hand but couldn't help but chicken out. Twice they rolled in those linens, but she couldn't tell if it meant anything to him.

"So, what's a lady got to do before you tell her a little about yourself? You can start with that lock pick kit if you want. Totally up to you." Wish smiled and felt her heart was as light as a feather as she wondered if she was too direct. Perhaps, *what're your favorite book?* would've been a better starter.

"Tell you what?" Joseph said calmly, looking ahead, before dashing home like a hare being chased by a coyote.

That was unexpected. Wish looked down at her heels, looked back up at his vanishing silhouette, sighed, and gave chase.

CHAPTER THIRTY-ONE

Mr. Dillinger zipped up his hoodie and looked out the kitchen window. A navy Honda Civic pulled up in front of the house, and a fellow dressed in dark tones emerged from the car and walked away with a key still in the ignition. He pulled out his phone and texted Ma to confirm the delivery. He then texted Mr. Karpis to ensure he'd meet him at The Dover in fifteen minutes.

He drew the small kitchen window curtains back together, removed the latex gloves from his hands, and tossed them into the bucket between his feet. If he'd learned anything from his brief stint leading Ma's cleanup crews, all would be as if they'd never been there. He walked out the door with the bucket in his hand, unlocked the trunk and tucked the bucket into the back corner; had to make sure there'd be enough space for Ma's golden boy. Any breaks or bruises to the things she liked often resulted in equal breakage and bruising to delivery personnel. He shut the trunk, walked back into the house and into the kitchen. He unzipped his duffle, made sure everything was in order, and zipped it shut.

The doorbell rang.

Mr. Dillinger's veins grew icicles as he slowly unzipped the duffle. He reached for his gun while keeping his eyes on the hallway, then tiptoed as quietly as one could on those aging floorboards.

He stepped out into the hallway with his pistol behind his back and stared at the door he'd left open. The car remained with the engine running, but no one stood at the door. He shut the door, pressed his forehead against it and laughed at himself. Perhaps he'd heard one too many tales of the dark realm that was Berkeley—the Den of the Proselyte—that Ma's soldiers had to learn to fear.

Myths, perhaps they were, used to toughen you up for the trials that usually accompanied furthering Ma's agenda; fables to keep you on your toes, which Mr. Dillinger consequently found himself standing on.

To the kitchen. Then to The Dover.

He turned away from the door and felt the icicles in his veins promptly melt away as all nine pints of blood gushing through his veins flooded his head in a hot burst as he came face to face with a dark figure wearing tinted desert goggles and a ski mask.

With his hands dipped in an invisible bucket of dried cement, and his foe too spry, Mr. Dillinger felt a harsh blow to his nose from the intruder's elbow, causing him to lose his balance momentarily, before finding himself standing at an angle on his right foot and left knee. His body felt like a bag of broken glass as he tried to lift his pistol up and fill his seemingly elastic evening guest with lead, only to find it kicked out of his hand, before the intruder laid him flat with a boorish knee to the neck, sending his face bouncing off the wall to his right and onto the creaky boards.

Retaining some modicum of his consciousness, Mr. Dillinger squinted in an attempt to gather any details he could on his rude trespasser, but a bright buzzing flash sent him into the light.

CHAPTER THIRTY-TWO

Charles got out of bed with his pillow and blanket in tow, opened his walk-in closet, climbed carefully into the hammock his mother had mounted to the wall for him, and tried to get some sleep. As cozy as his bed was, the heavy footsteps from his parents' room shook the floor and his bedframe. Not a lullaby many could doze off to.

On a positive note, his mother took her beatings in silence, and you could almost not hear his father's fists knocking into her. The sound of the backside of his father's hand clapping against his mother, however, dug through the wall like yodeling termites.

His mother was a perplexing creature. She could spend an entire afternoon running back and forth between the Home Depot, Target, and home, all to secure his hammock to the walls of his closet beyond a doubt, then she would choose a day to fix neither her bed nor his, despite knowing full well it would send his father into a frenzy.

Today, however, she seemed to operate with intentional neglect and Charles was left to stew in contemplation of her motives while fearing his father's impending fury upon her. Yesterday, she'd left both their beds disheveled and the sight of his father not battering her to the bone was a miracle. This very morning, on the other hand, she'd made both their beds, welcomed Lyla, left him in her care while she abandoned them for a few hours, returned home, kissed him on the forehead and proceeded to shake their sheets silly before his father had gotten home.

Their room possessed many sharp corners within its walls, not unlike many other rooms, and his father's rage produced a remarkable rate of stamina that made you wonder if his mother could emerge from that dark prison as anything more than a puddle of mush.

When Charles was much younger, such raucous nights were instigated by his father's desire to renovate his mother's sharper, dingier flaws, but this night wore an entirely altered façade governed not by his father's anger, but by his mother's underlying desire and design for something he could not yet put his finger on.

The thumping and trampling stopped, and he hopped quickly out of his hammock and back into bed.

Footsteps exited his parent's bedroom in silent motion and his door squeaked open. His father told his mother to go back into the room and she did, shutting the door slowly behind her. Moments later, a different kind of disturbing noise came from their room.

CHAPTER THIRTY-THREE

Mr. Karpis hid in the dark crevice between two houses across the street while waiting for either the tardy Mr. Dillinger or their target to emerge. He pulled his phone from his pocket to check the time; quarter to eleven. He shoved his phone back into his pocket and ground his teeth. Lengthy stakeouts were murder on your buns when in a car, but out on your feet, alternating between standing and hunching, was prone to making you want to impale yourself on one of those neighboring pretty picket fences.

His theories, as they stood, were as follows: at half-past nine, Mr. Dillinger's obsession with cleanliness had got the better of him, and he'd wiped the house down two times over. At ten, Mr. Dillinger, no more invincible than anyone else, found himself beset with explosive diarrhea. At half-past ten, Mr. Dillinger, relieved of his desire to leave the place spotless and his bowel ailments settled, would perhaps find himself sitting in the car, toiling to tune into a station worthy of a kidnapping.

On the cusp of eleven, with the formulation of his theories proving reliable only in killing the time, but unreliable in yielding the truth, Mr. Karpis arrived at the theory that would not flatter to deceive. Mr. Dillinger, at this very moment, was either one of two things: dead or soon to be dead.

Mr. Karpis sunk deeper into the crevice as he heard racing footsteps in the distance.

"Wait, hold on! Come on, please!" said Wish as she and Joseph arrived at the bottom of the stairs.

Joseph sat on the steps as she rested on the rails while they caught their breaths.

"You're faster than you look," he said, glancing at her legs.

"Track and field." She put her hands on her waist, looked up, and puffed. "You?"

He rested his elbows on the step behind him and pressed his back against the stairs. "Four white boys, but it wasn't like that. Well, sometimes it was like that."

Their target sat on the stairs while a chick stood by him. Mr. Karpis could not hear them clearly. Ma's boy stood up, put his arm around his lady, they went up the stairs together, she pulled a key from her purse and let them in Unit One.

Mr. Karpis took a deep breath. So, it was not his apartment, it was hers. He could always wait for him to go home, but from the looks of it, Ma's boy was headed nowhere but south. With Mr. Dillinger, the task would be simple: gut the girl and get the boy. Alone, Mr. Karpis did not trust that he could restrain himself from gutting them both, which in turn, would leave him to be fed to Ma's baler. He always wondered if it had been modified to crush human bones, or if they could all do that right out of the box.

He waited a few moments longer, then rose from the darkness and into the street.

Mr. Karpis climbed the stairs of The Dover and maintained a safe distance between himself and the doorsill of Unit One before pulling his gloves and switchblade from his back pocket.

CHAPTER THIRTY-FOUR

Mr. Dillinger's captor patted him on the gut twice. They then stood back up, pulled a pair of scissors from their back pocket, and cut his shirt off, leaving him exposed from the waist up while affording him the dignity of keeping his pants on.

The culprit tossed the scissors aside and proceeded past him to the back end of the spacious storage unit.

He could hear the clicking sound of buckles before his captor returned to him with a full-body, stainless steel hammer. They raised the hammer over their shoulder, poised to strike.

"You best review what the fuck you're thinking before you swing that shit around," he warned the tall, slender, masked figure.

The figure stretched the hammer further behind their shoulders.

"DON'T YOU—" Mr. Dillinger's pupils dilated at the sight.

The hammer struck his left kneecap violently before his captor paused.

Mr. Dillinger worked to soak in the pain, but his captor's pause was followed by a flurry of thumping swings at both his knees until he could hear his very bones shifting beneath his skin like shattered fragments of gliding marble, muffled only slightly by the sound of his own scream.

Cornelius tumbled out of his room with his backpack in hand and picked his phone off the kitchen counter. He cleared Wish's missed texts and opened Dr. Heller's. Nora had been found and the Richmond unit concierge would pick him up shortly.

His phone rang. He burst out the door, made sure he locked it, and turned to the hallway. He froze at the sight of his neighbor, Jenna, whose body was half-consumed by a hoodie twice the size of a man twice her size. This was the moment, as inconvenient as it was, he promised he'd commit.

"Jenna, good evening," he said with as bright a smile as he could muster, with the thought of Nora causing boils to grow at the back of his mind.

She nodded and retreated to her apartment slowly without turning her back to him. "Hey. Forgot something," she said, pointing her finger over her shoulders. Her door swung closed behind her.

Cornelius took a deep breath, tugged at the hem of his shirt and black hoodie, then dashed for the stairwell.

Mr. Dillinger grunted and struggled to catch his breath as his knees decked his veins with the song of agony. The clattering of metal against metal echoed from the back of the storage unit while his captor sifted through a container for their next tool of torment.

The clattering seized. He heard three quick leaps before grinding his teeth to suppress his body's unquenchable urge to writhe. He succeeded, and the sharp instrument jabbed deep into his back drew his attention from his throbbing knees.

The masked hellion stood before him again, this time grasping a bundle of sharpened steel skewers. They let them rain from their hand onto the concrete floor but kept hold of one. His captor stretched the skewer over their shoulder—Mr. Dillinger dreaded where it would land—and thrust the skewer forward, only to buckle mid-air and drop it.

The captor's elbow seemed to have twisted awkwardly and popped, causing them visible pain. They brushed their elbow while pacing back and forth to soothe themselves.

"You done?" Mr. Dillinger asked. "Going to fucking end this, or at least order us some pie while you decide?"

His evening host from hell turned their back to him and bent over to pick up the skewer they'd dropped, allowing Mr. Dillinger a glance at an unsettled thick red lock of hair poking out from under their collar.

"FUCK!" he grunted, as his captor's body twisted rapidly like a cyclone and stuck a skewer into his exposed gut.

Kyle parked the car across the street from the building, shut the engine off, and pulled his laptop from the sleeve under his seat. He brushed his hand over his thinning cliques of blonde still clinging to his scalp while flipping the computer open and powering it on.

He sneezed suddenly, and Cornelius looked at him with great concern from the passenger's seat. With his pasty anemic complexion, Kyle seemed almost a sneeze or cough away from the obituaries in the morning paper.

"She doesn't have much tolerance for this shit. Wonder what she's going to do with her?" Kyle sniffled, looking at Cornelius.

"Nothing. Dr. Heller won't lay a finger on her. She knows the deal," Cornelius said, tucking his fingers into his collar and centering it.

"You think she cares about you? You know how many of 'you' the doctor's got to deal with? You step out of line, put her and the rest of them at risk, and she'll put you six feet under; eight feet under, just for good measure." Kyle looked at his computer screen and began typing.

"Just our luck, then," said Cornelius, drawing his attention. "She's not a client yet." He opened the door and stepped out of the car. "Cameras?"

"Done. Fourth floor, K-twelve."

Cornelius tugged his shirt and hoodie by the hem and then dashed down the street and into the building.

He arrived at the unit shortly, pulled his mask and tinted desert goggles out, and put them on. His ear hovered an inch away from the sliding door. He recalled the anxiety he felt in the beginning when he'd used his first unit; his fear that the screaming was too loud for anyone not to hear, but here he was, in the company of none other than deathly silence.

Cornelius hunched at the center of the door, took a deep breath, wary of what he may see on the other side, and quickly pulled it open. Like a fox, Nora pounced and thrust a skewer through his left palm, wrestling him onto his back.

She sat up, looked back at the unit, then back down at him. She lifted his goggles slightly, saw his eyes, then got up and put her hands over her head in panic. She helped him up, pulled the skewer out from his hand, no less casually than one would a cocktail umbrella from a Mai Tai, and cupped his face between her hands.

Cornelius looked over her shoulder at the human-kabob hanging in the unit. The subject's knees were dripping with blood, with some twenty-odd skewers half-buried across his body.

The only thing he could think of was, *who the hell is he?*

For Dr. Heller, specifics mattered. *Kill or maim.* You also had to have a narrow category of people to subject to your urge. For some, it was tween cyber-bullies, online trolls, abusive spouses, chronic cheaters, drug dealers. You name it, it had to be fixed and definable. For him, it was anyone who took what wasn't theirs bar for desperate survival, and if it wasn't theirs and they took it, then he'd take something they'd miss from them.

Nora had piggybacked on his urge for some time now, and he worried she may prove to be the one Dr. Heller would find herself hopeless to help. The subject of her urge was quite broad. Too broad. There are too many of them—a few billion too many—and if you were one of them, that's all you had to be for her to want nothing more than to skewer you to death.

Was he a father, a good man, kept steady, went to work, paid his taxes, loved his family? Cornelius was not foolish enough to think anyone could ever be a remarkable saint. The haste with which Nora carried out her plan today, however, made it a challenge to accept that she'd somehow picked out an awful fiend with great accuracy from among the Berkeley masses who truly deserved such a fate.

She dropped the bloody skewer she'd stuck him with, turned and pulled the door down. She took off her goggles and mask, tossed them aside, and pulled her pen and notepad from her pocket. She flipped it open and wrote something down before both items were smacked out of her hands and onto the floor.

She looked up at Cornelius shocked and on the brink of tears as her cheeks turned red.

"FUCK." He turned his back to her. "Sorry." He faced her again. She reached her hand out to him. "FUCK." He turned his back to her again and took off his goggles and mask and tossed them aside.

She picked up her pen and notepad. She turned, and he tried to grab them from her hands, but she held firm. They struggled like school children fighting over a shovel and bucket in the sandbox before Cornelius pried them out of her hands.

Nora's tears began to flow as he snapped the pen in half and tore her notepad apart, dropping them at her feet. She'd never seen him in such a rage. She opened her mouth, but he knew she wouldn't say a word. Even in shedding tears, she was silent.

"Kyle's outside across the street. Go wait in the car. I'll finish this." She put her hands on his shoulders as he wiped her tears away. "I said, wait. Just a little longer. Please wait. She can help you, too. I don't…" Cornelius lifted her hands gently off his shoulders and approached the unit. He looked at her. Words seemed on the tip of his tongue before he slid the door up and entered the unit.

Cornelius hunched by the man and looked him in the eyes. *No, you can't tell a good person from a bad person from looking at them.* He stood back up, centered his collar, and tugged at the hem of his hoodie, then went to the back of the unit. There was a crackling of plastic sheets, before Cornelius jolted the back of Mr. Dillinger's neck.

Kyle sat up as a delightful silhouette emerged from the building and drew nearer. Black jeans, a black leather jacket, hair as fiery and full-bodied as his lava lamp, and lips as red as his own after a Kool-aid binge. He licked his fingers, elevated himself in front of the rear-view mirror, and brushed his eyebrows. He fell back into his seat as she opened the door and sat next to him. She sniffled and brushed her fingers under her eyes.

He cleared his throat. "You need a napkin?" He knew he had a box of napkins somewhere. He rummaged under his seat, where he kept more things than one should.

Nora raised her hand to stop his search.

"AC? Radio? Tough night, huh? Are we waiting, or does he want us to leave?"

Nora leaned forward and blew hot air onto the rear-view mirror, while Kyle glanced at her figure, before squinting at the mirror. There were squeaks, then she fell back onto her seat.

WAIT, the mirror read. She unzipped her jacket, tossed it in the back, and reclined her seat until she was out of sight.

"It's toasty in here, isn't it?" said Kyle. "I can cool it down."

He adjusted the AC knob, switched on the map light, sat back, and leered at her intermittently as the car's interior grew cooler.

Mr. Dillinger came to, and the prognosis of his evening deluded him no further. Industrial plastic sheets hung from the ceiling and covered the ground and all the walls.

Cornelius returned before him and set a chainsaw down.

The smile on Mr. Dillinger's face soothed Cornelius' guilt. Only a very particular ilk of person could find a reason to smile in such a circumstance rather than soil themselves and plead in a panic. They were either Nora, or they were the type who led such a life where they could appreciate such a doomed fate as inevitable.

Mr. Dillinger chuckled. "It is what it is, isn't that right, youngblood? One day you're hanging them, and the next day you're getting hung."

Cornelius' heart finally settled.

"Get me another hit of that." Mr. Dillinger nodded his head at the stun baton behind him. "Then do what you're here to do."

Cornelius and Nora sat in the back seat, him ignoring her while she blew hot air at her window and wrote to no reply. She stopped and sat back.

"Hey man, don't leave her hanging," said Kyle as he drove down University, not really sure why she didn't just speak.

"Can you please shut the AC off? It's getting a bit cold in here," said Cornelius.

"Did you have to cut him up or was he a smaller dude?" asked Kyle switching the AC off.

"If he fitted in the case, it wouldn't have taken me so long." Cornelius sighed and pressed his hands over his eyes while Nora crossed her arms and stared at the headrest in front of her.

The car stopped. Cornelius and Nora looked out the window.

"There's nothing to worry about. The boys will be in at dawn, polish it up, take the case to disposal, get rid of that car, and you're free and clear," said Kyle, looking at Nora.

She looked at him and produced the faintest of smiles. Cornelius looked at her, then at Kyle, and rolled his eyes. Nora got out of the car.

"Hey, hey," whispered Kyle as Cornelius stepped out.

Cornelius ducked back down.

Kyle looked past him as Nora stooped over to tie her shoes. "What's her deal, man? Are you two?"

Cornelius shut the door and walked away.

3

THE HOPEFUL

CHAPTER THIRTY-FIVE

Anson sifted through the suit rack, raking his mind for a reason to justify wearing a suit for his visit to the Nelson's that did not include impressing his crush… if that was a thing a grown adult could have. He pulled out a navy-blue suit and trousers, and the thought of wearing them made him want to smack himself. Unless he was a recruiter from Cal sizing up Charles as their new wide receiver, he had no business being welcomed into their home wearing such a suit. He put it away and drifted toward the tasteful khaki trousers and soft-toned cotton pullovers.

He had a family photo at home, the only one he cared to carry with him from those miserable days. In it, his parents were much younger. His father wore a pair of khaki-colored trousers and a white button-up shirt under a glacier-blue pullover, while his mother wore a red summer dress with a blue polka-dot print. You couldn't trust people. They lied all the time. A smile was a dangerous facade. He couldn't remember if the photo was from before or after his birth, but if his father was even a tenth of the man before as he proved to be after, then Anson would bet his memory of yesterday's ecstasy on his mother's smile masking nothing but terror.

He walked over to the cardigans and sat on the cushioned bench next to them. He buried his face in his hands. It was a simple thought, yet it proved practically impossible. All he had to do was wear something that would make him seem a better man in Mrs. Nelson's eyes, all the while making Mr. Nelson feel lesser without offending him. To accomplish this would've proved an easy undertaking for most. However, to achieve it without relying on the bravado of a suit, but rather, with a subtle yet communicative outfit that compelled Mr. and Mrs. Nelson to feel the things he wanted them to feel, seemed no easier than him trying to comprehend quantum physics.

Anson looked up as the air surrounding him started to smell like raspberries and sandalwood.

"You okay, hon?" asked the slightly bulbous, middle-aged saleswoman wearing a cozy knitted beige cardigan. "Aw, I know that look when I see it." She sat next to him, and he scooted over. "Someone take it, or they break it?"

He ran his hand through his hair and tucked a few strands behind his ear. "It's complicated."

"With those eyes and that face, it can't be. Follow me, Ol' Blue." She patted his shoulder and walked away. Anson got up hastily and followed. "Tell me, Blue, what's your lady do for a living?" They stopped in front of a large mirror at the far-right corner of the store. "What's her favorite color, movie? Where's she from?" She shot him a few more, realizing that the relationship was perhaps still budding.

He hadn't the slightest idea how to answer any of them. He looked at her as if she'd caught him with a bloody knife in his hand.

"You've spoken, you and your lady, Blue? This isn't a peeping-Tom type deal. Say it isn't so?" She looked up at him, her eyes praying he was less Bundy and more Sinatra.

He whispered something.

"Huh? Hon, you say something?" She took the smallest of steps away from him without realizing it.

"We've been intimate, but we haven't done much talking yet." He finally put forward his defense, and she crashed into him like a baby bear, hugging him by the waist-side in sweet relief.

Anson stood there like a rock, unsure how long to let this carry on before it started feeling weird. She let him go and her nametag popped off her cardigan and dropped to the ground. He hunched down and grabbed it for her. *June*, it read. He handed it back to her as she seemed to wipe a tear from under her eye.

"That's fine. We've all been there, hon. You meet someone and you just… well, you just want to turn each other into a platter and sample the works. Spent the summer of eighty-two with a man in a shack down in Cabo. Two of us shook off five pounds by the time they dragged us out of there." June's face turned from pasty to pink as she fanned herself with her hand. "My, oh my, it's a warm day, isn't it, Blue?"

Anson nodded and smiled with a blush. June stood next to him and looked at his reflection in the mirror. "Okay, so you don't know much, if anything about her, but I'll tell you something most men don't know." She pulled him away from the mirror and they sat on the bench by the dressing room. His interest piqued. Anson huddled closer. "You ever wear, let's say, a checkered black and green flannel during Christmas, or a mint pastel T-shirt on a hot summer day, and you see a woman, and she's also wearing a checkered black and green flannel or a mint pastel tee, and you feel this electricity?"

He nodded.

"We might not say it and it's mostly because we don't understand what the feeling is, but God, do we love it. It's like a silent telepathic signal that just tickles our heart when we see someone we're attracted to wearing something that matches what we're wearing. It's a very short connection we share in passing, but we love it." She stood up, and just as Anson was to follow, she put her hand on his shoulder and pushed him back down onto the bench.

"Now, Ziggy, I know when a man sees a woman he can't resist, he's helpless but to see straight to the warmth of her skin and contemplate the electric rush of her touch, but if you really love this woman, you must remember what she wore the last time you tangoed. Better yet, what she wore the time before last. Trust me, less obvious."

CHAPTER THIRTY-SIX

Wish closed her eyes while her heart raced, and a warm stream poured over her body and clung to it like a reassuring translucent cloak. She shut the showerhead off, stepped out of the tub and wrapped herself in her towel just as a nippy zephyr crept beneath the door and pricked her toes.

She stood in front of the mirror, her hair tossed over her shoulder, and met her own eyes. She hadn't anticipated the fun of the past two days, but for all the worries they allowed her to exorcise—if only for a moment—they'd sewn into her a fear she couldn't quite put her finger on.

She entered her bedroom just as Joseph slipped his socks on. He looked up at her from the side of the bed and smiled. "Where to?" she asked, leaning against the dresser.

"Going to check out the thrift store on University that you told me about last night. Need to get my apartment properly set up. Can't sleep here every night, right?" He stood, winked, and smiled at her, before grabbing his T-shirt from the foot of the nightstand.

"I'll grade you later and we'll see about that," said Wish, trying to sound like someone's grandmother, while wagging her finger and frowning at him comically. Unable to maintain the guise for very long, she burst into laughter. "Sorry, I just creeped myself out."

"Don't say that. I'd be up for round…" They both tried to remember how many times they'd turned the bed into a compact CrossFit over the very brief duration of their relationship.

"Three?" said Wish.

"Come on, four. Twice Saturday morning, then twice again last night. Trying to tell me something about my game?" He laughed.

"No, just feels weird. Didn't realize it. Kind of feels like it's been a week." She walked over to her closet and slid the door open.

"What're you up to?" he asked, walking into the bathroom, and running the water.

"Going to check on some friends down in Claremont." She ran her fingers through her hair.

"The ones who didn't show up last night?" He poked his head from the bathroom door as she stepped further into her closet.

"Yeah, just a little worried about them. They usually—" Wish felt hands clutch her by the waist, before finding herself twirled around and hoisted into Joseph's arms. He seemed to glide before he fell back-first onto the bed.

"What are you up to?" she asked as he ran his fingers through her hair. "You're going to get your fingers wet."

"I'm feeling this. How about you?" he asked.

She tapped him on the shoulder, he let go of her waist, and she rolled off. They sat up on the edge of the bed. "I don't *not* like it," she said, gathering her hair into a ponytail and threading it through a ribbon he could only assume she'd pulled from a crack in the space-time continuum because there were no pockets in that towel. "What?" she asked, as he appeared perplexed.

"Nothing."

She got off the bed and stood in front of him. "I like this, whatever 'this' is, but I need a little more than just what we've been up to before I can—"

He put his hand over his eyes and laughed.

"What?"

"Don't worry. I'm not going to pressure you to say it," he said.

"Say what?"

"You know. None of *this*," he said, waving his hands over his swimsuit area, "until we've done some of this." He made babbling ducks with his hands.

"I wasn't going to say that" she countered.

"Tell you what, text me later, around seven. Tell me where you're at and I'll be over."

"For what?" she asked.

He stepped in closer to her until their toes touched and lifted her chin. "Dinner." He kissed her forehead, and they stayed like that until one of them—neither would concede— silently passed gas.

CHAPTER THIRTY-SEVEN

Mr. Karpis stood outside and looked up at the office window. He ran his hands through his vivacious strawberry-blond hair as he reveled in his decision to wash out the ghastly dye Mr. Dillinger had ordered him to apply. If dead men told no tales, then their orders certainly didn't hold up posthumously.

He arrived in the waiting room—took the stairs, and put on his new green Sunski shades, for the hell of it—and was met with a glare as dark and as deep as the arrow-slits of an ancient Mesopotamian stronghold.

He approached the desk of the headscarf-adorned receptionist, neither of them uttering a word, and dipped his hand into his pocket. She reached her hands further under her desk while keeping her eyes on him before he pulled a card out and dropped it over her keyboard.

Rahma let go of the scimitar leaning beneath her desk and picked up the card.

It was Ma's calling card.

It had a soft beige, almost buttery finish with Twizzler-red borders, and at its center, embossed in dark Coca-Cola-brown, was a bucket of popcorn filled to the brim, with a plaque that read *Ma* at its center, also in Twizzler-red.

She extended her hand to him to return the card, but he took off his shades and waved in the negatory. "Got a glove box full," said Mr. Karpis, blowing air on his shades and polishing them before he hung them on his chest pocket.

She put the card down and pressed a button on the com. "Doctor, your nephew is here."

Mr. Karpis looked at her as though she'd just pulled a rabbit out of her headscarf. The light on the intercom blinked twice. Rahma nodded and pointed her hand at the door to Dr. Heller's office. He left her and stood hesitantly at the door, unsure whether he should knock or not.

"She is ready for you," she assured him. He nodded, looked at the doorknob—puzzled by how clammy his hands had suddenly become—then entered the office.

It was broad, with a large window at the other end of the room where the doctor's desk stood and where she sat at the moment. Closer to him was a sitting area with a couch, a rectangular, smoothly finished oak coffee table, and an armchair neither too plush nor too sparse on cushioning. On the table sat a plate of freshly baked cookies.

Dr. Heller looked up at him and he could see the strong familial bond she and Ma shared, despite the difference of their skin color and only sharing a mother. Some had it, but most didn't—eyes that commanded respect and dominated with a glance.

"Sit," she said, shutting the journal she had open and putting it away.

Mr. Karpis sat on the couch and eyed the cookies. She sat across from him, crossed her legs, and rested her back.

"The Proselyte?" he asked, just to make sure.

She smiled faintly. "Dr. Heller. Use that. Sounds better. Scares people less," she said, nudging her chin at him. He sat back as well. "You, done?" she asked, her words seemingly poking her visitor to sit up straight and avoid getting too comfortable.

"No, not yet. Lost a piece," he said, sitting up.

The doctor crossed her arms. "Mr. Dillinger got swallowed up?"

He nodded.

"You know by whom? Where?"

"No, he's just gone."

"Going home, then?"

He shook his head. "Not done here. I'll finish it up myself."

Dr. Heller sat up, arched her back, and shook her head. "No, you won't, boy."

He held her gaze as they sat in silence, before turning his head to the door as Rahma entered the room. She hunched and sifted through the cabinet behind the couch. He looked back at the doctor. She sat back.

"My sister knows what I expect from her when she sends you boys into my home. I need to know why you're here, how long you're going to be here, and if Berkeley eats a Mr. or a Mrs. Dillinger up, then Mr. or Mrs. Karpis must go home. Did she tell you boys that?" asked Dr. Heller.

Mr. Karpis nodded. "We know the deal." He hunched over abruptly to nab himself one of those cookies before hitting the road but felt and heard a sharp zip through the air just above his head. Still hunched—cookie in hand—he shot a look at the doctor.

"Rahma, close the window please, it's getting a bit cold in here," said the doctor, appearing tense for a fraction of a second.

He turned his head quickly toward the window behind her desk and saw that it was closed, just as he remembered it. In his periphery, he caught the sight of a long keen-edged shimmering object in Rahma's hands pointing toward the window along with her outstretched tense arms. Mr. Karpis sighed, and before Dr. Heller could meet Rahma's regret-oozing stare, he pounced, hurtled over the table, and buried the Proselyte in his shadow.

CHAPTER THIRTY-EIGHT

C harles felt his mother's hand brushing gently against his cheek as she eased him to wake. His eyes opened slowly to the sight of her smile—you couldn't tell for a second that she'd been kicked around like an empty Coke can mere hours ago. She kissed him on the forehead, brushed his hair into form with her fingers, then slowly limped away. You could always leave the face untouched, but for men with flaring tempers like his father, that surplus of rage usually translated into fracturing or breaking other things that could only be hidden by excuses.

Charles dried his face and joined his father at the breakfast table. His father looked at him as if to say, *what're you waiting for?* His mother wasn't too keen on him wandering around the kitchen without supervision, but his father often adhered to the principle of, *lose a finger now, learn to keep the rest tomorrow.* You were never a little boy, just a little man.

He got up and returned momentarily after climbing from the stepping stool onto the granite countertops, grabbing a plate from the cupboard, and loading it with some scrambled eggs and bacon strips. His mother often prepared his breakfast along with hers, in an effort to prevent him from one day clutching his chest and plunking into the ground, as she anticipated his father would, hopefully sooner rather than later. This very morning, however, she remained like a ghost by the window, flipping through a magazine.

"You want to say something?" his father asked. Charles' heart stopped as he feared a confrontation would erupt between his parents, before realizing his father was speaking to him. "Anything you want to tell us, son? Better we hear it from you than from your teacher," he continued.

Charles looked up at him and shook his head.

"Am I going to be happy?" he asked.

Charles nodded. "

What do they teach you at summer school, anyways? Thought it was just for those kids. You know the ones."

Charles looked at his eggs and bacon strips turning cold by the second, before feeling his father's fingers sinking into his hair and shaking it all up, drawing a quick glance from his mother.

"You're like your old man, you know. Hate getting grilled before getting fed." His father chuckled and returned to stabbing at his eggs.

Just as Charles impaled his first strip, he dropped his fork as his father stomped his foot into the ground, shaking the table. His mother put her magazine down, tightened the ice pack wrapped around her waist and walked over to the table to pick up his father's plate and wash it. His father cleared his throat as she rinsed the plate. She set the plate down in the sink, went to their boy's room and made his bed. Charles had chomped his way through a third of the eggs and strips on his plate when his mother returned to the kitchen sink.

"Go to your room, son," said his father as half a strip hung out of Charles' mouth. "You finish those coloring books your mother got you?"

Charles shook his head and put his fork down.

"Go finish them up." His father smiled, patting the back of his head.

He got up and made his way to his room as the faucet ran and his mother scrubbed away at the dishes. His father got up from the table, stood behind her and wrapped his arms tightly around her waist; she flinched for the briefest of moments before carrying on. He watched from his bedroom door as his father buried his nose in her neck while directing a beastly glare at him.

Charles closed his door and looked at the coloring books under his bed, before deciding to pull his Walkman out from the nightstand and popping in his mother's Manilow mixtape.

CHAPTER THIRTY-NINE

With the blinds at a quarter-pivot, the floor lamp unplugged, and only the light from the TV filtering through the room, Nora sat on the couch flipping through the channels, while Cornelius redressed his hand a little too tightly. As the red seeped through the dressing and with his eyes fixed on the TV, Nora swatted the roll from his hand and grabbed her pen and notepad as it unfurled on the ground.

TOO TIGHT. She put the pen and pad down, unwrapped the dressing, tossed the unsalvageable and started over for him.

"Thanks," said Cornelius, feeling a bit woozy. She smiled and continued diligently. It remained placid for a moment; the events of the past evening seemingly forgotten. "Are you ready?" he asked, flattening the wrinkles of his T-shirt over his abdomen with his fingers.

She nodded.

"With an open mind; it won't work any other way. You'll have to sacrifice some liberties if you want her to help you." He took her wrist as she secured the clip holding the dressing. She looked at him. "Don't play tricks with her. She'll probably scold you a bit for last night, but you've got to take it in, keep quiet and listen to her. She knows how to help people like us, and she'll find a way to help you. Okay?"

Nora stood up, swept her hair over her shoulder, smiled, and nodded. Cornelius got up and pulled the blinds back, flooding the room with the morning sheen.

Cornelius checked to make sure the door was locked as they stood in the hallway, then stopped as Nora walked toward the stairs. She turned and watched as he stood motionless in place.

"I'm forgetting something," he said, just as she tucked her hand into her pocket to grab her notepad. Cornelius patted his pockets and confirmed that he had his keys and phone. The two of them shared a puzzled look, as Nora, too, felt she'd forgotten something.

Wish turned the key, opened the door and dashed through the lobby and up the stairs. Her heart raced and blood swelled through her veins as she searched her mind for what may have caused Cornelius and Nora to miss her gallery opening the night before. Cornelius first arrived in her mind. What with the little he could actually feel, perhaps he'd forgotten to grab the wooden spoon and instead reached into a boiling pot to stir the noodles with his bare hands. Worse yet, perhaps he'd been chopping celery while watching the news, and failing to stop before hacking off one finger too many, bled to death without realizing his error. As kids, they foolishly marveled at his congenital analgesia as some kind of super power, but enough playdate accidents and much more had happened since that it had long loomed in her mind with severe contrasting earnest.

She stopped at the top of the stairs and pondered the unthinkable. Perhaps she was simply snubbed. Nothing was eternal; the Mayans, phone booths, Destiny's Child, and now, the gang who traveled the arduous path from Malcolm X Elementary through Berkeley High.

Wish stood at their apartment door. *Never!* She bellowed in her mind, refusing to allow time to chip away at their friendship. She huffed and pulverized the doorbell.

CHAPTER FORTY

Joseph entered the lobby as the fellow manning the box office nodded him in, then proceeded past the unemployed concessions stand before entering Auditorium One.

The lights were dimmed, and he noticed the screen was paused as he approached Ma, who'd been sitting in her favored seat at the center of row H. You couldn't see them, as Ma preferred the illusion that she was alone, but her boys kept watchful eyes on her from the shadows cloaking the exits.

He went up a few steps, then sat next to her as the big screen froze over Rick and Ilsa's lips joined passionately together.

Ma balled the napkin in her hand and tossed it to the ground before pulling another from the box next to her. Her eyes were pink, her nose red, and her tears left streaks on her make-up peppered face. She sniffled, blew her nose, then looked at him.

"You okay, Ma?" Joseph asked.

She nodded, smiled timidly, and put her hand on his shoulder. "Their love…" She looked at the screen, let out something along the lines of a cry and a laugh, then looked back at him. "Their love…" Her lips melted into a frown, and he could tell she was about to break out into the type of inconsolable agony her boys feared most. He put his hand behind her head and pulled her face into his shoulder. She began to cry, sending tremors through his bones.

A minute passed, and she pulled her face back up. She wiped the tears from under her eyes, grabbed another napkin, blew her nose, and tossed it to the ground. "It's so special," said Ma, grabbing another napkin and wiping his shoulder.

Joseph nodded.

She sat back and looked at the screen. "I want it, their love, but…" She looked at the baler at the bottom-right corner of the auditorium. "The men my boys find me, they don't love *me*." She brought her hands up to her chest and clutched them. "They just want me. And their father. Oh, how I loved him, but he never—"

"Ma?"

She wiped the tears from under her eyes. "I'm sorry, my love. I'm rambling, aren't I?"

"I love you, Ma!" shouted a voice from the shadows.

"Me too, Ma!" said another.

Two more declarations of love echoed from the shadows, bringing a smile to her face. She looked at Joseph and held his gaze.

Joseph smiled. "You know I love you most, Ma. No question." He could feel the others in the shadows trying to shank him with their glares. "What do you want to talk about?" Joseph asked.

"Boys!" Her voice rang throughout.

"Ma?" flew from the shadows.

"Leave us, please."

Clicks sounded from every corner as they left and shut the doors behind them.

"Is everything alright, Ma?" Joseph asked.

You'd never know if you hadn't spent most of your life under her thumb, but you could throw a T-shirt, a pair of Levi's, and a Jansport backpack on Ma and she'd fit right in at any sorority without a moment's doubt. No one the wiser of the masses she governed, and the crystals she trafficked throughout the nation and parts of the world. She'd go to classes by day and chat up the cartel czars by night. She was blessed like her mother, to be twice the age of any freshman, only to appear two years their junior. Perhaps it was that and her much-revered wit that enchanted her followers to buy into her ways, but Joseph knew, as did her sons, that it was so much more.

She held her hand up, snapped her fingers, the screen turned dark, and the auditorium was lit. She rested one hand on her knee, turned over the other, and asked for his hand. Joseph put his palm over hers.

"This business we deal in, it comes with many trials, you know. After putting my father away, and after growing up witnessing the way he handled himself and his people, I vowed I'd do it differently. That I wouldn't run this business or my people through fear. I think you feel the same way, don't you?"

"Of course, Ma. But I don't think anyone's doing it the way you do it."

She smiled. "They can't, but you can."

Joseph's heart skipped a beat and his hand instinctively tried to pull out of her clutch, but she held firm as though she'd expected it.

"Don't fret, my love." She set his hand free. "The time will come, but it's not tomorrow, and it may never come, but if it does, I need you to step up. I look at my boys and I see my father's temper. I could never hand them the wheel. I could never let fear govern our business again. My father, like the cartels, the Mafia, the Triads, he chose fear disguised as respect to keep his crew and his neighbors straight, but I chose—"

"Love," said Joseph. "But Ma, your boys, they'd—"

"Don't you worry about my boys."

"What do you mean?"

"They'll back you, they promised."

His heart raced as though his kidneys were chasing it down with a chainsaw and a barbwire bat.

Ma grabbed a napkin and patted it on his forehead. "Baby, this is not a ceremony, this won't all be yours tomorrow. Just keep up with the numbers and the routes." She tossed the napkin on the ground, raised her hand, and snapped her fingers. The room turned dark again, and the screen grew bright. "Want some popcorn, hon?"

"Sorry, Ma, maybe next time." He smiled.

She put her hand over his ears, pulled his head in, and kissed his forehead.

Joseph locked the door behind him, stuck a chair under the knob, and rushed into his room. He ducked under his bed, pulled out his roller, and unzipped it.

When it came to Ma's boys, fight or flight wasn't nearly a consideration for those who'd known them. The question you asked yourself was, how far could you fly with the bones you could get away with unharmed?

Joseph opened his closet and felt a blow to his chest that propelled him into the side-frame of his bed. He looked up at the giant army boot encased foot that had emerged from the shadow before it was set down, and Ma's second oldest stepped out into the room. He wondered suddenly—as his chest pulsed—if the boys had been so aggressive all their life because they'd begun to lose their hair so early.

"Grayson… hey," said Joseph, coughing as he helped himself up. "My bad, man, didn't see you in there. I think your brothers are looking for you, but I lost them back at the deli."

Ma's boys weren't skinheads, nor were they Klansman, despite what one heard on the streets. Joseph, more than most, knew that, but then again, you learned a lot about those with whom you've bunked with most of your youth while spending all your youth racing out of their reach, only to get your ass handed to you before bedtime. It was simple: they were large, cursed with their grandfather's temper, lost out on their mother's looks and wits, had deep-set eyes the color of jaded sapphires, and began balding at fifteen. That the ladies weren't too keen on them, due in part to their less than delicate mannerisms, and with their mother prone to breaking a few of their bones should they touch any of her girls, they'd often find themselves with vast reserves of pent-up aggression than most people would know what to do with. Credit was due to them, however, for their rotation policy, that allowed each one of them a weekend out of the month to leave town in pursuit of tail where their reputation didn't precede them and where anyone other than their mom ran the prostitution rings.

"Hey, pal." Grayson lifted Joseph by the collar. "There's something on your nose."

Joseph's eyes widened. Perhaps it was because that'd been the thousandth time he'd heard that phrase and knew it was often followed by someone's forehead or fist pulverizing his nose. He flipped the switch just as Grayson smiled and stabbed his neck with the taser he'd pulled from the underside of his bedframe.

Worryingly, Grayson seemed to be holding his own as the current coursed through him, his grip somehow growing tighter, but soon enough, he dropped to the floor like a clunky suit of armor.

A thud against the door sent a shiver down Joseph's spine. The boys had followed, and unless he had an industrial bolt cannon under his bed, Joseph had little time to debate what to take and what to leave behind. He felt a tight grasp over his ankle as he made his way to his closet. He looked down at Grayson mouthing something.

"Danish or scone?" Grayson seemed to be asking. "Excuse me, sir. Sir?"

Sir? Grayson didn't have those kinds of manners.

"Huh?" Joseph looked up at the barista. "Sorry, what was that?"

"Danish? Scone? Anything savory for you today?" she asked.

"Both, and an Americano, please."

He sat at one of the tables outside and looked at the building across the street. He directed his gaze further up at the fourth-floor windows and wondered how he'd make his approach.

Ma warned her boys against wandering into the Den of the Proselyte without her consent. More so, unless your name was Mr. Dillinger, you were to never meet the Proselyte in person. The way Ma regarded Berkeley; you'd think you were wandering into Caracas. The chief difference between the two was that Ma often recommended her boys try the pabellón criollo down in Caracas.

Joseph took a bite out of his Danish and sipped his mocha frap as he watched a fellow with curly hair and a lady with hair no less voracious than the California wildfires stop and stand in front of the building. He wondered if they were there to see the Proselyte, or perhaps they were shopping for office space. The two of them looked at each other. The young lady pulled a notepad from her pocket, wrote something down, and stuck it in front of the fellow's face, to which he shook his head.

Joseph averted his gaze as she quickly turned her attention toward the café. Her companion uttered a few words, and they were soon in the building lobby.

CHAPTER FORTY-ONE

Dr. Heller sighed while she stood over Mr. Karpis' corpse, garnished with the cookies she had Rahma fetch from the café across the street earlier for her first session with Nora. She got the table back on its feet, then walked over to her desk. She unscrewed the silencer from her gun, unlocked her desk drawer, and stowed them away.

Rahma set her scimitar down against the wall and went to shut the blinds. She returned to the shelves behind the couch, removed the painting from the wall, unlocked the safe, and pulled a small black box with a toggle switch out.

They both returned to either side of Mr. Karpis' corpse—his chest still seeping from the three holes the doctor had sunk into him. She nodded, and Rahma flipped the switch. Dr. Heller looked at her wrist, counted ten seconds on her watch, then said something.

Rahma shook her head.

Dr. Heller looked down at his body and shouted a very popular expletive, and Rahma smiled and shook her head. She couldn't hear a thing. They nodded at one another. Rahma exited the room, closed the door behind her, and felt a shiver as she noticed Cornelius and Nora sitting in the waiting room. They both smiled at her.

She took an imperceptibly deep breath to calm herself and approached them. They stood. "Cornelius, I'm glad to see you." She shook his hand. "Nora, welcome." She embraced Nora, whose hands remained by her sides, taken by surprise.

"How's Dr. Heller?" he asked, looking down at his collar as he straightened it, then tugged the hem of his shirt.

Rahma frowned. "She became ill, unfortunately. So sorry I didn't have a chance to let you know. She left only a few minutes ago."

Nora held her notepad up at Cornelius. *We can leave?*

He sighed, bit his lips, and nodded, noticing the joy Nora labored to keep under wrap.

"I'm so sorry. Just this morning, she came in, began to prepare for your meeting and started to feel sick," said Rahma, waving her hand over her throat. Cornelius shot a quick glance at the doctor's office door. "She asked me to reschedule you for tomorrow." She put her hand on Cornelius' arm while looking at Nora. "She would like to see you as soon as possible without any further delay. Tomorrow morning, I promise."

"It's okay. Thanks, Rahma. We'll be back tomorrow." He smiled.

"Wait, before you leave." She hurried to her desk and returned with a Yogurt Park card with nine holes in it. "It's nice outside. Have some frozen yogurts, go to the park, yeah? It will be fun." Rahma held the card out and Nora graciously accepted, despite wanting nothing more than to go home and have those walls stand between her and them out there.

CHAPTER FORTY-TWO

Anson parked the car and shut the engine off. He looked into the bag and felt his heart rising like a soufflé in his chest in anticipation of his visit to the Nelsons in the evening. He reminded himself, as he felt his insides grow too giddy for the occasion, that it would not be a date, and that Mr. Nelson would be there, so deodorant and the mildest touch of his cheapest perfume should suffice and offend no one.

He climbed the stairs, perhaps with a little overload of gusto in his heels, and found his toes suddenly caught in between two steps, throwing him completely off balance, and leaving him to brace himself for the thumping dive his back would endure as he tumbled down the concrete steps.

Anson opened one of his eyes while the other remained pinched, still bracing itself for the sting of the fall, and looked up at the neatly trimmed young fellow whose arms he'd fallen into.

The fellow smiled at him. "Whoa, buddy, that was close. You okay?"

Anson grabbed the rails and lifted himself out of the stranger's arms. "Thanks." He looked over the fellow's shoulders and down the stairs at what could have been. "You just saved my evening."

"You're welcome, man, it's becoming a habit," laughed the stranger.

"I'm happy it is. You new here?" asked Anson as they both headed up the stairs.

"Yeah, moved in Unit Three around Wednesday night."

"Really? Didn't hear a thing, and I'm in two."

"Not much to move, just a roller. Brought in a futon and a couple of other things Friday afternoon. Joseph, by the way," He extended his hand as they passed Wish's and stood in front of Unit Two.

"Anson." They shook hands.

"So, I don't mean to be intrusive, but I try to make sure I'm aware if I just earned myself a favor. You never know what you'll need and what someone can do for you. You said I saved your evening. What are your plans tonight if it isn't a bother?" Joseph looked at his fellow neighbor coyly while leaning against the rails.

Anson looked down at his keys with a smile on his face as he twirled them around.

"Special plans?"

"Yeah, sort of met someone," Anson replied. "Feels awful and great at the same time, you know. Don't want to get ahead of myself, though."

"I feel what you're saying, man." Joseph smiled while glancing at Wish's door.

"Staying put or are you here—"

"Staying put, I hope, but you never know," said Joseph.

"Have any family or friends around?"

"No family. Trying to get away from all that. No friends either, but I've been hanging out with—"

"Wish, yeah," said Anson, nodding his head. "Figured it was you after you said you were in Three. Seems like you're getting along well." He grinned.

"My God, man, sorry." He buried his face in his hands. "You never realize."

"No need to apologize. The walls here are just thin enough. I don't know what the nature of your relationship is, but if it's headed for something serious, I can tell you that Wish is good people."

"You two?"

"No, it's not like that. Borrowed some latex gloves from her a few times. Guess living next to a BPD CSI has its perks—that, and they've got everything you'd need to get rid of a body." Anson laughed. "She also assists the medical examiner on occasion. She tells me that's the role she really wants. That's a very bright woman you're spending time with, don't mess it up."

"I know she is. I won't mess it up." Joseph looked down and chuckled, trying to mask his shock at her profession. "Alright, man." Joseph moved away from the rails. "I'll leave you to it. Need to get ready too. Wish and I kind of flew through the bases, so we're going to start over and have dinner tonight."

"Enjoy," said Anson.

"Later, man."

CHAPTER FORTY-THREE

Cornelius stepped out into the hallway, then rushed back to the staircase, hiding behind the wall as Wish sat outside their door. Nora pulled the spoon out of her mouth and dipped it back into her frozen yogurt. He slumped to the ground and bounced the back of his head gently against the wall.

The gallery opening was the yucky dread he felt turning in his stomach all morning as he scoured for what was unsettling him. Nora's Saturday night misadventure had led them down a dark path, but it had less to do with the late-night chopping and packing, and more to do with the small vessel of rage camped outside their door right now.

Nora poked her head from behind the wall, dropped her yogurt cup—which Cornelius managed to catch—and fell against the wall across from him. Swipe left for phishing and junk texts, but never your friends, was the sacred doctrine.

They strategized silently while Cornelius labored to unwrinkle his shirt in his awkwardly seated position, which made his attempt a futile one. He looked away from his shirt and at his dressed hand. That they were in the emergency room was a ready-made alibi, but the texts they had ignored and left unopened circled their necks like a noose. They were not the kind to let the text bubble grow without responding, but the mood of last night left them to seek comfort in the lullaby of silence.

He pulled out his phone, opened his texts and read the two Wish had sent. She was not one to bludgeon you with endless follow-ups, but if you'd endured the trials of Malcolm X Elementary through Berkeley High together as they did, then she'd sure as hell show up at your door.

Nora looked at him, despair in her eyes, as Cornelius gasped a little too loudly. He turned his head toward the top of the stairs like a rusty corkscrew.

Wish hunched over at the top of the stairs. "You know, I wonder," The two of them looked up at her, their heads stiffened like dried cement. "If I blast you with vinegar—not the kind you top off your salad with, no. I want to do more than just stink you up. The high concentration type people clean their boats with—would it kill you or just turn your bones to Jell-O if I soak you in it long enough? I already know the answer, as I should. Think about it before running. Medical examiners know where to get the good stuff, and CSIs know how to stage the perfect crime scene."

Wish smiled and Nora realized there was a realm between surprise and fear she didn't like very much—but it was not fear, it could never be fear for her, just fear-adjacent.

CHAPTER FORTY-FOUR

Lyla shut the drawer and went over to the shelves to alleviate her concerns and make sure all the files were in order for the manager who'd be replacing her. She sat back in her chair, put her purse on her lap and pulled out a pack of Newports. She popped the pack open, stared at the filters for a few seconds, then flipped the lid shut. She put her legs up on her desk, leaned into her chair, and looked up at the ceiling fan.

She tried to remember her life before Mrs. Nelson, then decided not to, before quickly relenting. There was her husband, whose mind had forgotten that trimmers existed not a year into their marriage. No longer the slab of Greek's finest hubba-hubba inducing man-God with the ability to weave words into liquid gold that she'd fallen for all those years ago. There were the endless lines of college sophomores—burdened by heavy course loads while trying to figure their life out—that she began seeking out in every campus neighboring bar when she'd had enough watching her husband spend more time wrestling with their dog than rolling back to their steamiest best hits and making new ones.

As much pleasure as she gave and got with all those women everywhere from stuffy dorm rooms, inherited Honda Civic's, unattended supply closets, the occasional childhood bedroom when the parents were local but out of town, to bar bathrooms, Lyla relished what came after, when she could just doze off atop them, soothed to sleep by their soft skin as they stroked her hair; but none ever shook her to the core of her desires like, Mrs. Nelson. The only point of fear she had about their relationship was that she didn't even know the first name of the woman she loved, but there was a promise between them, and she held onto that. She knew Mrs. Nelson wanted to tell her so much more about her past before she could feel a deeper trust between them and reveal every part of who she was.

Lyla sat up and grabbed a napkin to wipe her forehead with. There was a line most people thought impossible for them to cross, but when they met their Mrs. Nelson, suddenly it was possible. Likelier than anything else. She hunched over her desk, closed her eyes and envisioned it. The woman she loved, Charles, and the Wyoming sky.

Lyla closed her office door, bag in hand, and walked over to the girls as an elderly man wearing a red and blue fedora exited the store. Ashley appeared to tuck an envelope away as Lyla approached.

"Ladies," said Lyla, glancing at the dark crevice Ashley had tucked the envelope into as the women looked at her sorrowfully. She put her bag down, opened her arms, and they embraced her. Ashley let go, but Brianna continued to cling. Lyla wrapped her other hand around her. "Come on, you'll be fine." She felt Brianna's hands loosen around her waist before letting her go. Brianna wiped tears from her eyes while Ashley patted her on the back and smiled. "Now, don't tell me you're not happy. I know you won't say it, but with Nelson also leaving a lot more clients are there for the taking."

"She didn't even say goodbye. Bitch left a note." Brianna fought back tears.

"I'm going to miss the bitch too," said Ashley. "Come on babe, you won't be able to make a sale with your mascara looking like that."

Ashley caught Lyla glancing at her envelope while picking up her bag. "Sorry, I know we're not supposed to have family over for personal matters while on the clock, but my uncle was just dropping by to deliver some money my mother sent over. He's in town and…" Her hands fell by her side.

Lyla waved it away. "Don't, that's fine, I get it. Just make sure you let the new manager know in advance next time. They haven't gotten wasted with you at the Starry Plough yet, so…" She covered her lips with her hand as they quivered, dropped her bag, and opened her arms again.

Lyla tossed her bag in the trunk of her car, locked it up, jumped in the front seat, and cast her purse aside. She shut the door, put her hands over her face, and took a deep breath.

With the engine running and her heart no longer in Berkeley, she put her foot on the gas, then screamed and slammed the brakes as a knock came from her window. She looked over at the fedora wearing old man waving at her from the other side. She smiled as she rolled down her window.

CHAPTER FORTY-FIVE

Dr. Heller looked at the reflection in the dark screen of her iPad and straightened her bronze, balance scale-shaped brooch. She unlocked the screen and continued to watch the muted footage of Nora doing her worst to the late Mr. Dillinger in the cold, hellish confines of K-Twelve. She looked across the waiting room at Rahma, who'd pulled open the drawer on her right, looked down into it with a grin, then returned her gaze to the computer screen and continued to scroll.

Rahma's father had earned his keep in the desert with his scimitar, and she had little interest in following in his footsteps—not that it was even permitted by law for a woman to do that job in the Kingdom, and that was an exclusion she was happy to abide by. Kyle would be over later in the day and her silencer would no longer find itself rolling around in that drawer lonesome, and she'd be done scrolling through the web reading gun specs and thinking about her aim.

The office door opened. Dr. Heller and Rahma looked up as the cleaners exited the office with an elongated metal case for the second time in twenty-four-hours. Mr. McClure's ashes would soon have company. They nodded to her, then descended carefully down the stairs on their way back to their van.

A notification popped up on the screen of the tablet letting Dr. Heller know that her phone was shaking senselessly in her desk drawer with a familiar name. She folded the case over the screen and walked to her office, when a stranger suddenly arrived in the waiting room, bringing her and Rahma to a halt.

The stranger smiled at them. She wore a large glossy pink rain jacket, jeans, and a pair of Birkenstocks, looking to be on the right side of her twenties, but on the wrong side of insomnia evident by her bloodshot eyes.

"Hey, what is this place?" she asked.

Dr. Heller nodded at Rahma then entered her office, shutting the door behind her. Rahma handed the stranger a card and explained to her that they offered life coaching services, but that they were regrettably not taking on any new clients now.

Dr. Heller sat in her chair, set the tablet down, and opened the drawer. She watched the phone shake incessantly, hoping it would fall silent before picking it up. "Baby girl," she said, then chuckled.

"Well, in my defense, none of your lackeys wiped your ass before."

"Margo, I'm not going to say it. You can have your boys running around calling you Ma. Whatever gets you going, but I know you better."

Dr. Heller grunted. "Let's move on. What do you want?" She swiveled her chair around to the window.

"The old man is gone. Couldn't tell you who did it."

"Could've been. You know the deal when you send your boys here. I can't guarantee you their lives."

She swiveled back around, leaned back into her chair, put her feet up on her desk and crossed her legs. "Karpis was me," she said, then immediately held her phone away from her ear as Ma bellowed in shock and agony.

You'd think she birthed him herself, Dr. Heller thought.

"You okay, Margo?"

She could hear her sobbing on the other end. "Margo, baby girl, the boy wasn't cut out for it; Dillinger requested the termination."

The crying halted immediately, as if on cue. "He sent me a message, then paid me a visit. Hadn't seen him since I left."

She sighed. "I told you; it could've been anyone, and no, they didn't use one of my units. This was a rogue. Could've ended up either way. Dillinger wasn't a pushover."

Ma stayed silent for a moment. Dr. Heller took her feet off her desk and hunched over. "I'll miss him too, Mar—"

"Yes, you don't forget the man who snuck you *Dante's Inferno* and taught you those numbers."

"Margo, I've got stuff to—"

Ma fell down the dangerous rabbit hole many knew as nostalgia. Dr. Heller pressed her phone up against her ear with her shoulder and walked over to the painting on the wall. She set the painting aside, unlocked the safe, and pulled out her calendar.

"Yes, still here." Dr. Heller floated her marker over the calendar and landed it on the eleventh. She crossed out the initials and put *NF* down on the twelfth.

CHAPTER FORTY-SIX

Anson stood in front of the wooden gate with a bottle of wine in one hand and—for no reason other than it looked fresh and smelled like hope—a baguette in a waxed paper sheet in the other. He paused outside the gate a few minutes ago, his body growing warmer and his scalp moist. He looked down at his attire; a blue cardigan, a daisy-white button up, a pair of dark blue jeans, and a pair of oak brogues. Suddenly he felt overdressed, even after giving himself ample time in front of the mirror at home to decide. It seemed to have emboldened him a little too much.

He pushed the gate open, ascended the steps, and stared at the door of the Nelson's home. He set the wine and baguette down by the door, grabbed his phone from his pocket and examined his face. Assured, he tucked his phone away, knocked on the door, and lifted his offerings.

He heard steps approaching, a few clicks, then light fell upon him and a man he could only presume was Mr. Nelson stood at the door. Anson felt his fingers tickle as he reveled and resisted a grin, while the soft-featured, yet unremarkable fellow stood before him.

Mr. Nelson remained muted as he seemed to examine Anson's get-up, having anticipated for no apparent reason, an academic indentured to tweed and bifocals and much thinner hair.

"Welcome," he said, having allowed sufficient time for Anson to sweat through his shirt.

He stepped aside, and Anson observed Mrs. Nelson like one does an endemic wonder, sitting at the table adorned in the less jubilant tones of a black turtleneck and a long, dark-green skirt. She presented a contained smile.

Jordy leaned against the counter as the sky lost its bright disposition. He continued to spin a pack of Pall Malls while awaiting the stroke of ten when Mr. Nelson would arrive, and he'd be released back into the night with the other creatures to dread tomorrow. The packet slipped from under his finger as his hand shook due to the loud arrival of Boyd.

"Nelson! You around, man?" He sauntered in wearing a large red jersey with a name on the back Jordy couldn't quite pronounce. "Hey man, where's the boss?" Boyd stopped at the counter and pulled his phone from his pocket.

"Home. He'll be by to close later," said Jordy, getting the Pall Mall back under his finger.

"You into soccer?" asked Boyd.

"No. Won't change the channel if it comes up, but not really a sports person. Maybe some college football if I have to."

"Man." Boyd tucked his phone away. "You need to check it out. My wife's family came in from Ethiopia last night wearing these shirts." He pinched the jersey. "Going mad about this World Cup final today. Spain against the Netherlands."

Jordy nodded, wondering that if he killed himself, if Boyd would be able to man the counter until Mr. Nelson got in.

"Anyway, man, they're kicking that ball around like it's nothing but a homing pigeon, and those tackles were nasty. The Spanish and Dutch have beef between them?" he asked as Jordy pinched his lips and tried to think of something. "Well, hey, it isn't Lakers and Celtics, but I might take a look at a game or two if I'm feeling it." Boyd looked around the store as silence fell.

Jordy stood in place, nodding with his hands in his pocket.

"Alright, man, I'll see you around. Have a good night." Boyd nodded and left him to his Pall Mall twirling.

Anson looked up at the ceiling gasping for air, tears swelling in his eyes as he forgot how loud he was laughing before he got a hold of himself and looked back down at Mr. Nelson wiping tears from his eyes. You thought you'd heard them all, then came the man you wanted to hate, with the most obscene joke you'd ever heard and wouldn't fathom repeating to anyone, but something you'd chuckle about every now and again and immediately scold yourself.

He glanced quickly at Mrs. Nelson, who seemed less than amused, and bit his tongue. She caught his glance, grabbed the pitcher, and poured him some more water. "Sorry, sorry, I wasn't quite sure where that was going until too late. Who came up with that? Never mind."

"Don't be, it's a good one. Heard it from one of the boys back at the docks when we used to live in San Francisco," said Mr. Nelson, putting his fork down and sitting back.

Mrs. Nelson picked up her plate and left the table with an odd limp in her step—Anson just realized he hadn't seen her move from her place since he got there. Mr. Nelson shot her a fleeting sharp glare, almost surprised that she'd gotten up."

"Hon, sit!" he said to his wife, almost a little boorish, as though he'd forgotten Anson was there, before adjusting to a milder tone. "Hon, you know you're not supposed to move with that pain. I'll clear up the table, okay?"

She froze in place with her plate in hand between the dining table and the sink. Too many seconds had passed, causing Anson to turn blue from holding his breath and wishing it would end before she returned to the table with a smile on her face.

Mr. Nelson looked at Anson. "Put herself in a weird position last night when she was sleeping and woke up with some tightness in her lower back and hips." He put his hand on her hip. "Going to Highland tomorrow so they can take a look at her."

"I'm so sorry, why didn't you tell me?" Anson half-rose out of his chair. "We could've done this any other time."

Mr. Nelson grabbed his wrist and helped him back into his seat. "No, no need. She's fine. Aren't you, hon?" Mrs. Nelson smiled and nodded. She seemed oddly fine with it, her smile brighter than the one she welcomed him with earlier. "Anson, go sit in the living room. I'll clear this up and join you in a sec, alright?" Mr. Nelson gestured over to the living room.

"Hon, would you check on Charles? See if the boy's okay, see if he needs anything."

She nodded, got up and limped to his room, as Anson watched her with great pain clutching his chest. He got up and headed to the living room just before Mr. Nelson could find a reason to question the way he looked at his wife. He joined him a minute later with a tray of wafers and some Minute Maid.

"So," said Mr. Nelson, sitting across from him. "My boy, is he doing well? Summer school, isn't it still for those kids? You know the ones."

Anson chuckled half-heartedly.

"Well, not really, it isn't, although a lot of folks still perceive it that way. Yes, we've got a few students who need to make up for their struggles during the semester, but honestly, there are more kids in it to set themselves up for success for the upcoming term. They've done well, but their parents want to keep up that momentum and not have them fall into the summer slump." Anson hunched over, grabbed a cup, and took a sip.

"Charles is doing well. He picks up on things quickly, you know. He follows instructions and doesn't cause any trouble, but…" He searched his mind for the right word while Mr. Nelson fixed his eyes on him like laser beams. "He's a tad bit aloof," he said, pinching his fingers together. "He'll communicate with me when it's one on one, but in groups, he disappears, not because he's unsure, but mostly because he's too nervous or scared to interact more freely."

"How?" asked Mr. Nelson.

Anson's eyes widened. He wasn't sure what he meant.

"Any examples?"

"Well," Anson put the cup down and sat back, "I do an activity with the kids, having them describe shapes and their angles, basic stuff. Charles obviously—"

"Need to use the can?" asked Mr. Nelson.

Anson suddenly became conscious that his foot had been doing the stuffed bladder dance. He looked down at it and smiled nervously. "Yes, actually." He got up.

"Next to the kitchen. The blue door." He pointed out the living room.

Anson slipped into the kitchen, past the dining table and found the blue door in the corner a few feet off a beige door, left barely an inch ajar. He entered the bathroom and time hastily stood still. Mrs. Nelson turned away from the mirror and looked at him. She stood there in her skirt and an embroidered floral bra, with her turtleneck tossed over the toilet seat.

He looked at her, horror filling his eyes as he bore the sight of the once smooth, colorless scape of her body that he could still taste on the tip of his tongue, bruised, and battered like milk mixed with transmission fluid. He'd seen it all before. It was less sleeping at an awkward angle and more finding yourself between a wall and the wrong end of a relentless fist. Either that or the Nelson's slept on a shrapnel-stuffed mattress, and Mr. Nelson had impenetrable skin, but Mrs. Nelson didn't.

"You get your fill, pal?" asked Mr. Nelson, sending a cold pulse up Anson's spine, as it appeared Mrs. Nelson was about to say something.

"Yes… I mean, sorry. I wasn't—"

"Hon, let the man use the bathroom before he soils himself," he said.

Mrs. Nelson put her turtleneck back on, Anson stealing a glance as she pulled it over her head, before she passed by him, brushing her hand ever so slightly against his thigh. She followed her husband to the living room.

Anson sat with his elbows over his knees on the toilet seat lid and flushed the toilet again, hoping to buy himself some more time. He looked at the reflection of his forehead in the mirror, then grabbed a sheet of toilet paper and patted it down. Should he leave? Impossible. He knew for certain what the life of the Nelsons was like. He'd lived it, he still had nightmares about it, and he couldn't run away from it this time. He could not convince himself that his fists were smaller than his father's. That his own anger would whither before his father's coked-up rage. That had he stood up to his father, the authorities would have pulled both his body and his mother's out from the basement freezer. This was different. He stood taller than Mr. Nelson, his fists were larger, and his love for Mrs. Nelson trumped anything he'd ever felt before.

He stood, tucked his hand into his pocket, then pulled it back out. It'd get messy if he called the cops and Mrs. Nelson stood by her husband's side. He'd have to get her and Charles away from Mr. Nelson's control and to the police station if he were to succeed in ending this.

He stood in front of the mirror. He had to get out. The longer he stayed in the bathroom, the more irked and suspicious Mr. Nelson would likely be when he did. The time was now, and the decision was made.

He washed his hands, splashed his face, and dried them with a paper towel. He stood an inch away from the door and waited for his heart to calm but accepted that it wouldn't anytime soon. If anything, it would soon beat faster and harder. He opened the door, clinched his lips, sharpened his gaze, and proceeded. He looked at Charles' bedroom door but decided not to have the boy witness whatever was about to happen; better to have Mrs. Nelson get him when they left.

As Anson walked back to the living room, he felt an odd sobriety overcome him. A light gait in his steps. A powerful bulge in his arms and chest. His heart calmed as he arrived back in the living room. He looked at Mr. Nelson and smiled, then passed by him, approached Mrs. Nelson at the other end of the couch and took her hand. Her husband looked at him as though he'd just stuck his hand up her skirt right there and then.

"You okay, pal?" asked Mr. Nelson, looking at their hands clasped together.

Anson looked at him with as austere an expression as he could conjure and nodded. "We're leaving."

Mr. Nelson's eyebrow rose sharply. He put his cup down on the coffee table and stood between them and the foyer. "Alright, pal, leave then." He gestured to the foyer without moving an inch.

Mrs. Nelson stood up, her hand still in Anson's, and kept her head low. He held her hand tight, walked around the coffee table, Mr. Nelson moved a few inches, and they met again.

Anson moved forward until the two men were a hair away from each other, each of their stares fixed on the other. He took another step, just short of stomping on Mr. Nelson's toe, and felt the man's hand pressed against his chest. Mr. Nelson remained silent and shook his head. Anson grabbed him by the wrist.

CHAPTER FORTY-SEVEN

Lyla parked the car on 55th just short of the underpass and turned the engine off. She opened the glove compartment and retrieved a Ritz-cracker sized remote control with a glowing red button. She held the control tight in her hand with her thumb hovering over the button. She sat back, felt like she was in a coffin, then sat up and hunched over the steering wheel.

Last time she'd felt this way, there was a ten-pound book on her lap, an hour had passed since the exam had begun and she decided to hell with the pantsuits, mahogany, and a life of lawyering, the big money was in diamonds. If she knew one thing to be true, the only thing she was better at than selling dreams was cajoling the pants off most Berkeley Law scholars who gave her serious Julianna Margulies vibes. She realized shortly after flunking out, that she was born and bred for law, and it filled her with dread and despair.

It all mattered not, however, for it was law be damned again the moment Mrs. Nelson walked in for an application shortly after Lyla's promotion from sales to management. It was kismet, as she found herself with the supreme power to utter, *you're fucking hired*—those exact words occurred mostly in her head.

Lyla sat back, the thought of Mrs. Nelson soothing her heart. She looked at the narrow house across the street. The

Nelson's was on 56th. She grabbed the control and pressed the red button. Thunderous booms sounded throughout the neighborhoods several blocks down in every direction. Lyla buckled her seatbelt, sat upright, and watched as the porch lights of the narrow house across the street lit up.

Anson's back stung as he rolled off the collapsed coffee table under him. Mrs. Nelson shrunk into the corner of the living room as her husband barked every obscenity under the moon at her. "You sleeping around on me!?" he bellowed, veins bulging over his left eye and forehead. The sound of his voice pinned her back.

Anson got on his knees as she brushed by him, failing to grab her by the wrist and convince her to stay behind him. She passed by her husband, walking in hesitant, small steps before he smacked the back of her head, making her wobble and sob as she retreated to the kitchen and out of sight.

Anson swept Mr. Nelson's feet as he charged in for a kick and sent him falling onto his back. He got off his knee, lifted his host by the collar, and charged into the kitchen, catapulting him onto the dining table.

As Anson bore over him, Mr. Nelson swung his forehead into his nose, losing the clutch on his collar, then grabbed a chair and swung it at him. Anson dodged out of the way before Mr. Nelson swung and released the chair at him, forcing him to duck for cover and watch as it flew over him and bounced off Charles' bedroom door.

Distracted by the chair momentarily, Anson found himself at the wrong end of Mr. Nelson's foot landing against the side of his head. Without a moment's reprieve, as though his head was suddenly made of stone, Anson lunged at Mr. Nelson and shoved him against the kitchen counter, the two of them tugging at each other's collars like it was the only thing standing between them and falling off a cliff.

Both men froze simultaneously, Anson feeling the abrupt shiver crawling from Mr. Nelson's fingers onto his, as they both heard what he could only assume was the hammer of a gun being cocked. He turned his head slowly as he felt Mr. Nelson's grip on his collar loosen and watched as Mrs. Nelson pointed a gun at them, likely with her husband in mind.

Anson loosened his grip and suddenly felt her husband's clutch tighten around his collar, before feeling himself flung around and shoved against the kitchen counter. Anson caught his grin for a fraction of a second as Mr. Nelson rolled out of the way, then he flinched as he heard a loud noise and saw a flash. Mere seconds passed before it sounded like a parade of canons had erupted into the Oakland night. He looked down and saw a growing pool of red seeping through his shirt. He put his hand over the hole in his chest. He looked up at Mrs. Nelson, tears streaked across her face, then saw another flash and felt his stomach burn and grow tight. He took a step toward her, then felt his head rock back as if he'd been hit in the face with a brick and felt the weight of his body plunge to the ground unassisted by his violently severed reflexes.

With his left hand sandwiched between his chest and the kitchen floor, and his right hand—he had no idea where the hell it was at this point—Anson tried to get one last look at Mrs. Nelson, but neither his head nor his eyes would budge. The coldness of the kitchen floor seeped through his cheek, and it was as though he'd fallen asleep in a warm bath gone harshly cold.

Mr. Nelson put his hand over the gun as it shook in his wife's hand. She let go of it and watched as blood pooled around

Anson, then looked away to her boy's bedroom door. Mr. Nelson put the gun down on the dining table and looked at the front door.

"Get me Ma's burner, quick," he said.

She rushed to the bedroom and returned to him with the phone.

Mr. Nelson turned to Anson's corpse, flipped open the phone, and dialed. He felt a sudden stinging burn in his back and feared he may have twisted it badly with all that excited movement. He continued to dial but felt the burning spread and grow more severe. His throat began to tickle, and his hands started to tremble. The phone slowly slid out of his now numb hand and his basic motor skills faded quickly. He turned to his wife and fell to his knees. Her hands were as red as the cherry Lifesavers he knew she hid beneath the sink. Her eyes were still wet with agony, but he felt excluded. He fell over and tasted the steely red in his mouth as the sharpness of the instrument plunged into his back became more pronounced. The adverts were true. It could cut through anything like butter: a can of soda, a smoking pot roast—and now, unquestionably—several inches through muscle tissue well past its prime, and into his liver.

His wife stepped out of sight and into their bedroom.

Charles standing in front of his bedroom door wearing his raincoat with his backpack on, earmuffs over his ears, and a pair of taped-up shades over his eyes would be the last thing Mr. Nelson would ever see.

Lyla could still hear the popping in her ears long after it had faded and the scrawny old man in the paper-thin robe returned to the narrow house and flipped the porch lights off. As sirens sounded in the distance, she felt a shiver of joy overcome her as Mrs. Nelson and Charles emerged by the narrow house and crossed the street hand in hand.

She tossed the control back into the glove compartment and unlocked the doors. Her hands tingled as the back door opened and Charles hopped in, waving at her while his mother secured him to the car seat. Mrs. Nelson shut the door behind him, then jumped into the front seat, tossed a pair of earmuffs and a pair of duct tape-sealed shades in the glove compartment, then finally looked at her. Her eyes were red, her face smelled like rain, and her lips were pursed so tight to avoid crying uncontrollably.

Lyla looked at Charles in the back seat before feeling herself tugged into Mrs. Nelson's embrace. They let each other go as the sirens passed behind them, the two of them looking ahead before catching a glimpse of Charles in the rearview mirror as he dozed off.

CHAPTER FORTY-EIGHT

Realizing he'd gotten off the bus a little too early, Joseph began his walk up Shattuck. He passed by Venus—that couldn't be right? He was pretty sure Wish had said Jupiter, or was it Saturn? She'd told him the name of the restaurant, then went off on a tangent about the menus at the other two restaurants, coincidentally named after planets. She then pointed out the fun fact that if you connected them on a map, you'd get an acute triangle, and how cool it would be if it was not a coincidence. She hesitated, then shared her bizarre theory with him. What if the connection between them was not a coincidence but part of a larger global seal put into place by occult guardians of Earth to shield the planet from rabid alien civilizations who'd been trying to sneak through and colonize us for centuries? He imagined that if she somehow had any time to spare between her career as a CSI and medical examiner's assistant, and her art, that she'd probably use it to write books.

As Wish hadn't been awaiting him outside Venus, he'd try Jupiter next, hoping she'd arrived earlier than he did and would save him from making the rounds of the acute triangle that kept humanity from its grisly demise. He'd already started sweating as he drew two blocks closer to Jupiter and dreaded the stamp of the awful pit stain. He stopped outside a burger joint, entered, dropped a fiver in the tip jar, and asked for the restroom key.

Fresh-faced, Joseph crossed the street and relished the sight of Wish standing outside Jupiter. Just as he was about to approach her, a large fellow in a manual wheelchair asked around for assistance with getting pushed over to the bus stop but received little attention other than a few sideway glances.

"Hey man," said the man, noticing that Joseph had paused among the constant motion. "Help me out real quick. Trying to get to the eighty-eight."

Joseph looked across the street. It wasn't too bad, despite the fellow having at least a hundred or so pounds over him. He nodded, got behind the wheelchair and pushed with all his might, while the fellow used his feet to try and ease the pressure on him.

It's moments like this that you discover what your workout regimen is really made of, thought Joseph as they finally arrived across the street, and he pushed the fella up onto the sidewalk.

"My man," he said, "this isn't it. The eighty-eight stop is by Wells Fargo." He pointed at the end of the lengthy block.

Joseph nodded and began the second half of their journey, pushing with all his might and lamenting his loss to the tip jar.

Having delivered the man to his destination, he jogged away to the sound of the man's praise and prayer and wiped his forehead with the back of his arm. He awaited the signal to cross while counting his blessings for having at least worn a dark enough T-shirt for the sweat stains to remain covert enough although the impending odor was inevitable. He looked across the street at Wish as she continued to wait for him, scrolling through her phone. A gentle breeze ruffled the bottom of her soft-toned red summer dress when the signal turned from orange to white, prompting him to race across the street, then steady his steps as he finally arrived.

She caught him in her periphery, put her phone away, turned and smiled.

"You look great," said Joseph, wiping his forehead again with the back of his arm. They both leaned in for a kiss, paused, then Wish planted a quick peck on him. "Not feeling warm?" he asked, looking at the short leather jacket hugging her shoulders, then admiring her cute toes and peach-toned strapless heels.

She shrugged. "It's not that warm tonight. Then again, none of us selflessly work up a sweat as much as you do before a date." She smiled, glancing at the bank.

He smiled, put his arm around her—regretted that immediately and pulled it away—and in they went.

They were led up to the second floor amidst the loud evening crowd and were seated by one of the tall windows.

"Did you make a reservation?" he asked, finally feeling his body cool down as he sat back.

"No, I got here super early and scared everyone off." Wish smiled and brushed her hair over her ears.

"Really? You didn't have to; we could've gone somewhere else." Joseph hunched forward.

A waiter arrived and handed them each a menu. "Drinks?" The waiter grabbed her notepad from her apron.

"I'm good, I don't drink," said Joseph.

"Really? Neither do I," said Wish, a little too excited, making the waitress tilt her head and smile at them with adoration.

"I'll be back in a few, you two." The waiter left them to it.

Having enjoyed their dinner, they both looked out the window in surprise, as everyone else seemed unconcerned by the distant booming noises. Fireworks, perhaps, but they had quite a raucous bang to them. Fireworks, they decided, then returned to their dinner with a tinge of apprehension. Joseph put the crust down, wiped his mouth with a napkin, and sat back.

"How was it? Any favorites? I've never ordered for anyone else before."

"The dip was great, I really enjoyed that. What about you, any favorites?" he asked.

"I love the garlic wings and the Cassiopeia. Pizza isn't usually my thing, but I like it here, and the Cassiopeia is a winner."

Joseph steepled his hands together and leaned in. "Ready whenever you're ready."

Wish grinned. "You're not being interrogated or anything, I just want us to"—she leaned in closer— "get to know each other in nonphysical ways," she whispered, then sat back. "Don't get me wrong, I enjoy that part plenty, if anything, it's my favorite, but it'll be better if we get to know each other more, or at all." She laughed nervously.

He smiled and nodded.

She leaned back in. "This is only a cliché because, I mean, it's always about the origins if you want to get to know someone. So, I guess, let's start with where you're from."

"San Francisco."

Wish laughed out aloud as if it was a hiccup she didn't see coming. She quickly kicked her embarrassment to the curb.

"Are you serious?"

He nodded and tried not to laugh at how flustered it made her. It didn't seem like a big deal to him that he hadn't crossed countless city borders before arriving in Berkeley.

Wish's phone buzzed in her purse. She pulled it out.

The screen lit up with a text headed, *BPD*, and an address under it.

"Is everything okay?"

She rolled her eyes, sighed, and got up. "I'm so sorry, but I have to go."

Joseph got up. "You have to?"

"I wish I…" She paused and laughed. "God, this sucks, but I really do. When the guy whose job you so desperately want has the number of two assistant MEs on his phone, you answer, and you run. I'm just realizing this is the first time you're hearing about what I do for a living."

He put his hands on her shoulders, leaned in, and kissed her. Still peeved by fate and its design to drive a stake through her friendships and now her love life, Wish did the only thing she could imagine would be the equivalent of flipping it the bird. Before he could step away, she pulled Joseph in closer and gave him the kind of kiss that makes a man feel like he's hanging upside down in the rain with a mask half over his face, breathless, but still conscious for no other reason than the current caressing her lips and stroking his, and also because that type of kiss was good for only ten seconds lest she wanted to kill him.

Joseph fell back into his chair, and watched as she raced out, crossed the street, and jumped into one of the cabs opposite the bank.

CHAPTER FORTY-NINE

The old man turned left from Shattuck onto Kittredge and proceeded past the downtown public library before descending the blue steps and arriving at the dark café doors. He pulled the key from his pocket and entered.

He looked at the corner of the café where she sat, her pink raincoat like a fluorescent beacon in the darkness as she flipped through the espresso machine manual. He looked behind the counter and found the young, pierced, purple-haired barista where he'd left him, manic on the floor, knees to his chest, in tears as he looked at the tiles in panic as if they'd been crawling with slimy baby slugs.

The old man removed his fedora, set it down on the table and took a seat. He unwound his scarf from around his neck and undid the buttons of his coat when she joined him at the table in the middle of the café. He put one leg over the other, grabbed the paper from the table, and began to flip through it.

"Where is she?" she asked, tossing the manual over the counter at the barista and making him whimper.

The old man looked at her. "Who?"

"Ashley. She isn't coming back with us?" she asked.

He shook his head. "Ma wants her to stay. I delivered her bonus for keeping an eye on Mrs. Nelson and left. Miss her, do you?" he asked, pointing his eyes sharply at her.

"No, I just miss not being around you. Necesito dormir," she said, looking over at the counter and yawning.

"Then sleep. Ashley and I are no longer partners. It's me and you now, so get used to it, dear. Ma's orders."

"I'm good. I'll sleep when you're dead. It can't be too long now. I don't plan on having your voice in my head, waking up thinking termites are crawling up my ass." She looked him in those gray, mirror-like eyes. Of all the Mr. and Mrs. Dillingers at Ma's disposal, why did she have to be partnered with him?

"Have you completed your report, Ms. Karpis?" he asked.

She nodded. "Mr. Dillinger—"

The old man shook his head. "Ma needs the real names on the report for the records."

She sighed. "Mr. Shaw is confirmed dead. The Proselyte's boys removed his body from one of her units in Sacramento and sent him down to the burners in Oakland. Looks like he found himself at the wrong end of one of the doctor's sick puppies. A red-headed puta."

He nodded and scratched his chin. "Go on."

"Mr. Warwell is also confirmed dead. He stepped into the Proselyte's office about noon today and never came out. Two hours later, the cleaners arrived and left. No sound. No echo. Poof." She rolled her fingers into fists and sprung them open like fireworks. "Is Ma going to let this fly? The Proselyte canceling one of her boys?"

"Mr. Karpis… Mr. Warwell was approved for termination. Mr. Shaw requested that service from the Proselyte himself. You must not delude yourself. If Ma bestows the name Karpis upon you, it means she sees promise in you, but at the end of the day, we Dillingers are responsible for shaping you into one of us. Should we deem you lacking in character to carry the name, it is we who are charged with your disposal; by our own hands or an external contract." He finally put the paper down, uncrossed his legs, and leaned in. "But do not sweat it, young lady. I see Ms. Dillinger in your future, should you continue to show promise. Anything else?" he asked, sitting back, and crossing his arms.

"I stopped by her office and—"

His eyes lashed at her like bullwhips. "Your promise is fading, Ms. Karpis. Have you not familiarized yourself with Ma's booklet on Berkeley etiquette?"

"I have but—"

He proceeded rather ceremoniously. "'The only officers, hitherto, granted lease to hold audience with the Proselyte, shall bear the Dillinger name and none other.' You foolish *clown*!" He rose from his seat, his fists bunched up. Mr. Dillinger took a deep breath, then sat back down. "Mr. Karpis earned what came to him, and I fear you fail to comprehend how lucky you are to have left untouched. Nonetheless," He rested his back, more at ease. "What intel have you managed to retrieve?"

"Well—"

The barista whimpered again from behind the counter, unprovoked.

"She's calling herself a life coach." Ms. Karpis pulled a card from her pocket and dropped it on the table. "Dr. Heller, Ph.D. Did la bruja actually graduate from anywhere?"

He picked up the card. "You would be wise to watch your language, dear. You see, some people come into this world with such inborn gifts that render such institutions and distinctions inept to define their talents. The Proselyte and Ma are such. This world is remarkably pliable to people like them." He put the card down.

Ms. Karpis looked at the café doors as loud pops echoed in the distance.

Mr. Dillinger smiled and put his fedora back on.

"Are we really just going to let her get away with it?" she asked.

"It is Ma's will that we allow that woman's plotting to bear some fruit, but not entirely. She will not be getting away. She still owes Ma too much."

Ms. Karpis rose and stood at the door, looking up at the night sky, half-expecting to see fireworks. "So, what are we waiting for?"

"We must first wait for Mr. Nelson to bleed to death. Ma has found that he has grown fickle. Then, we are to await Mrs. Nelson to come to us." Mr. Dillinger stood behind his partner, causing her to shiver and turn.

She looked at him and sighed. "You planted a suggestion in that lady's head, didn't you?"

He smiled. "Mrs. Nelson likes her women rugged and her men pretty. I caught up with her lady love on her way out and suggested she do what is best for all parties involved. I'm certain she'll do the right thing."

"And him?" She looked at the counter, casting a shadow over the barista.

"I suggested that, come dawn, he should boil some water, stuff a funnel down his gullet, and filter some peaberry before the early birds get in."

Ms. Karpis' eyebrow poked at him, unsatisfied with his level of transparency.

"I may have stipulated that bleach would serve better to filter the peaberry. No one enjoys filthy coffee beans after all." He relented.

"Isn't it going to draw too much attention?" She questioned Mr. Dillinger's zest for the macabre.

"We'll need the attention here if we want to conduct our last survey before leaving town, dear. We'll probably take a peek at the Nelson's before heading back home."

Ms. Karpis brushed by him and grabbed the newspaper from the table. "What about the crystals beneath the floorboards and the nosy neighbor?"

Mr. Dillinger picked up his scarf from the table and wrapped it around his neck. "As fate would have it, the boys just picked up the shipment the other day, so the floorboards shall tell no tales. Regarding the Nelson's nosy neighbor, he's a nice fella who works in Bart patrol. I chatted with him earlier and suggested that he should hop down on the rails with a wet cloth and bucket and welcome the Fremont train with a good scrub. You shouldn't neglect cleanliness. Filth is a horrible sin."

CHAPTER FIFTY

"So, what's your deal?" asked Kyle as the car headed down the I-880, his question whisking the grin of fantasy off Rahma's face as she continuously peeked into the inner folds of her coat at her new firearm.

She looked at him, her expression giving the answer her lips had little interest in uttering—such was the only strategy when dealing with someone you've met on numerous occasions and, without fail, have been constantly bothered with the same question.

Kyle glanced at her, then back at the road. "You've never felt like taking that off and like, letting your hair fly with the wind?" He wagged his head as if he'd had the uber-curled locks of Kenny G flowing from his barren scalp.

"I have a hairdryer at home," she said, looking out the window.

"You're telling me you've never wanted—"

She shook her head. Silence held for the briefest of moments as the car exited at thirty-eight and continued on High Street.

"Any celebrity crushes?" he asked.

She shook her head again. "From the street merchant in Riyadh to the coked-up oligarch in the Ritz-Carlton, men are all the same. You?" she asked as the car turned onto 46th Avenue and stopped short in front of a large, dirty, teal-gray warehouse.

"That's a loaded question, but I'll start writing and get back to you next time. Unless you want me to wait out here? I don't really have anywhere to go."

"That won't be necessary," said Rahma, pulling the door handle.

"You sure?" asked Kyle. "It's pretty rough down here."

"The van's inside. The boys will give me a ride back to Berkeley," she said waving as she left the car.

She unlocked the smaller door next to the towering gate and entered the warehouse. She flipped the switch and lights flooded the large vestibule where the van remained parked in front of a second gate with a smaller door built into it.

Rahma approached the driver's side of the van, where the sound of the rumbling engine continued. She reached through the window and switched the ignition off. Perhaps they'd just arrived, but if that was the case, then the cleaners must have made a stop first, and Dr. Heller wasn't a fan of stops when there was a corpse rotting in the back, no matter how odor-proof the metal case was. She walked past the front of the van, approached the second gate, and entered through the door.

A dimly lit space extended in front of her, made visible by the fading lights hanging high up from the ceiling. On either side of her, constructed storage units lined the walls, six on each side, leading up to the two incinerators at the furthest end of the warehouse, housed in a massive, checkered cube of cinder block and red bricks.

As Rahma made her way toward the incinerators—one of which remained open, releasing a wave of heat while the metal case sat beneath it—her phone buzzed.

She stopped and pulled it from her pocket. Dr. Heller. She answered.

"I am well," she said. "I'm here."

"Looks like it," she said, resuming her path toward the incinerators.

"They haven't done anything too concerning yet, but I'm not ready to blink. Salwa is keeping an eye on them." She arrived at the incinerator and shut the feeding door. "She's keeping both eyes on them, of course. One eye on the old man and one on the small lady."

Rahma turned and felt the stench of his bloodied lips ride his breath and brush up against her cheeks.

"It's Karpis, like tarps, you bitch!"

Faster than one could plead for mercy, Rahma let her phone slip, grabbed him by the shoulders, swung her forehead into his nose, stomped his toes, sent him tumbling with a kick to the groin, and swiftly unsheathed her pistol from her coat and pointed the barrel at his forehead.

"That fucking hurt," said Mr. Karpis, grunting under his labored breathing.

"You mean more than the three bullets in your chest?" Rahma kept her hands steady, despite her heart pounding.

"In my defense, the doctors told my mother I was born with shifty organs. Don't remember what they called it, but things in there kind of just creep around when I'm moving," said Mr. Karpis, waving his hands in a circular motion over his chest.

She cocked her gun. The head was always best. His brain couldn't have much room to squirm around in there—and she was pretty sure it was just a one-in-a-million chance that he survived rather than anything to do with shifting organs.

He held her gaze.

She waited, but her finger wouldn't budge, and the bullet wasn't autonomous enough to leave the barrel and do what was best for the world. She put the gun down and sheathed it back into her coat. "The cleaners?"

"It's called a feeding door, you know, so I fed it," he said, looking over her shoulder at the incinerator.

Still, she thought, *shifty organs or not, the body certainly couldn't survive that much blood loss*. Rahma held her hand out to Mr. Karpis. "The Proselyte has a special place in her heart for survivors, fighters and talented… death dodgers, if you will. Would you like to meet her?"

Mr. Karpis looked at his chest, then at her hand. "I'm pretty sure we've already met, and from what I remember, it got a little wet, and not the good kind."

"It's different when she takes notice of your value," she replied.

Rahma held her fists out to him then flipped them and opened her palms. Her left palm held nothing while a bullet sat on the palm of her right hand.

4

THE GUARDIANS

CHAPTER FIFTY-ONE

Cornelius exited the 19th street Bart station utterly embarrassed at his verbal entanglement from a minute ago when he'd accidentally said, "execute me," instead of, "excuse me," making a crowd of teenagers who'd been blocking the staircase leading out to 19th street break out into loud laughter. Granted, his true want was probably a quick execution anytime he was stuck behind a crowd of slow walkers on a sidewalk, stairs, or in a hallway, but now he'd be stuck gasping about the embarrassing moment sporadically for at least the next week. In truth, his subconscious slip was less to do with the young crowd and more to do with his inevitable approach to meet his brother, whom he hadn't seen or heard from for nine months. He couldn't remember the last time they had a get together—if he could call it that—without matters boiling over between them.

As Cornelius approached the alleyway where his brother had arranged for them to meet, he tried to imagine, with much futility, what things would look like if they weren't such different people. Rather than meeting in an alleyway, they'd meet on the steps before the scenic Lake Merritt, and they'd spend hours walking around and catching up, without even the slightest idea of how many rounds they'd made of the lake. Then, perhaps, they could end their walk on Grand Avenue and step into

Enssaro Ethiopia for dinner, wrap up their catchup like a smooth role of injera, hug, and try not to let nine months pass before checking up on each other again.

Cornelius arrived at the mouth of the alleyway sitting across from a Cultural Center and between two residential buildings. There was a barred black gate in front of the alleyway, which probably led to the parking for the building to his right. He approached the gate and noticed that the lock was missing. He reluctantly pulled one side of the gate open and entered the alleyway. He walked to the end and confirmed that it led to parking spaces. Unsure what to do with himself as he arrived a few minutes early, he returned to the alleyway and leaned against the cold bricks of the building.

As his mind begin to wander into a simpler past before his brother shattered their mother's heart, and their mother took her own life soon after, two men appeared and opened the gates. A box truck—that looked much too big to back up into the alley—started doing just that. The sides of the truck hovered a hair away from the exteriors of the buildings with its loud beeping echoing throughout. If no one made a fuss about him loitering in the alleyway earlier, Cornelius thought, they sure would now. However, instead, he noticed that the few alley-facing windows that had their blinds open were quickly shuttered. The back of the truck stopped a few feet away from him, followed by a burst of pressure released by the air brakes.

Cornelius stood away from the wall he was leaning against and had a bit of a jump scare as he noticed a van suddenly blocking the other side of the alley that led to the parking spaces. His heart settled as the door of the truck rolled open revealing quite a well-furnished space with a couch, TV, carpet, lights, a mini fridge, and plenty of other conveniences. It was like a professionally decorated guest bedroom that had been relocated from a penthouse and into the back of a large box truck.

Archibald stood there looking down at him with a smile. When they'd last met nine months ago, it was in a shabby motel room his brother was staying in that Cornelius was coincidentally near as he drove down highway 1 on his way back to Paolo Alto from Santa Cruz after a meeting. Had his brother not reached out at so opportune a moment, they'd probably have gone almost two years without seeing each other.

"Nelly, baby, it's been too long," said Archibald with his arms extended wide. Noticing his brother's hesitance to take the handle on the side of the truck and get up there, he sat on the edge of the platform and jumped off.

Archibald clapped his hand on his brother's shoulder and gave him a tight hug.

A woman appeared at the mouth of the truck and sat on the edge of the platform.

"Hey, Nelly. You've been good, baby?" she asked waving at him, throwing him a wink and a kiss.

It looked like his brother and Shanice were still going steady since Cornelius first met her in that motel room. Back then, the pair of them were dressed a bit more modestly. His brother wore a tank top and jeans, and Shanice wore a tank top and baggy boxer shorts. Whatever they'd been up to, they looked ragged and weary back then, and whatever happened since, they appeared remarkably reinvigorated. They both wore rugged leather jackets and casual tees paired with jeans. His brother smelled like he looked. Confident. He imagined that Shanice did as well.

"Yeah. I'm doing well, thanks," replied Cornelius shyly, giving Shanice a flimsy wave.

"I didn't realize you and Nora moved up to Berkeley, baby brother. I was thinking we'd meet somewhere around Old Paola Alto until I called to set this up, and you told me about your move. You, okay?" Archibald asked, rubbing the fingers of his right hand together making the universal sign for money.

"Yeah, we're perfectly fine," replied Rubix in a jump at his brother's insinuation. "We just bought a building in Claremont so we could be closer to—"

"Woah, baby, you heard that?" said Archibald proudly, looking over his shoulder at Shanice. "My baby brother bought a building in Berkeley," he said, elevating his arms like wings either side of him and turning his body full circle to face Shanice and then back to facing his brother.

"I heard, baby!" replied Shanice, looking playfully down at her swinging feet dangling over the platform. "You just hit me up when you're ready, baby boy, and I've got a list as long as both my arms of some fine woman who'd snap you up just like that," she said with a giggle as she snapped her fingers.

"You see his face, baby? This boy cracks me up," said Archibald in a laugh as he clapped his hands together at the sight of the perplexing smile cum grimace on Cornelius' face.

"God, I love him more and more every time I see that face," said Shanice, throwing Cornelius another kiss.

"How about you?" asked Cornelius. "I'd hope you're looking better and doing better because you've found a better path, but given where we're standing," he continued, looking around the alleyway, "I'm guessing your hands are still in the very same jar they were in the last time we met, and it seems that jar is paying up, so you're likely never going to let it go until it costs you more than it's given you."

Every bit of humor and sprightly energy evaporated from the air as Archibald's facial expression hardened and his jaw stiffened.

"My man, do you know how many empires came up and broke down before we got here?" asked Archibald thrusting his finger upwards to the sky and swiftly downwards at the concrete they stood on. "The Romans, Byzantines, Ottomans, the Qing Dynasty, the Soviet empire, the French empire. Every one of them told their people that their ways, their ideology was the right path to lead them to a good life, and every one of them fell due to any combination of political instability, economic decline, zealous military overreaching, but you know why they really collapsed? Because they didn't seek to govern their people to the good life, they just wanted to control them, so the few at the top could relish and bask in the excessive life made from all the good lives they promised and stole. These empires, dynasties, and ruling ideologues lasted anywhere from a decade up to a thousand years, my man, and we're not even accounting for the roots that birthed them," concluded Archibald, turning his back to his brother for a moment.

"Baby," said Shanice, "I don't mean to disrespect your heat, but real quick, we can skip foreplay later, I'm good." She fanned her face with both her hands.

Archibald blew her a silent kiss and turned back around.

"All I'm saying, my brother, is that people have been studying this shit, and they've been studying hard," said Archibald more calmly as he relaxed his jaw. "Every century, the beast gets bigger, Nelly. Do you know who the beast is?"

Cornelius shook his head.

"Us," said Archibald. "Society, the people, and the bigger the beast gets, the new bourgeois motherfuckers—"

"Language!" Shanice cut him off.

Cornelius felt a powerful warm pulse in his chest as he watched Shanice patting her currently flat belly.

"Sorry, baby," said Archibald, looking over his shoulder at Shanice with a sincere smile, more with the stretching wrinkles of his eyes than his mouth.

Archibald exhaled calmly.

"All I'm saying, baby brother, is that the stage actors are new, but their intentions are no different than their vanquished predecessors, but what has changed is the playwright, the director, and the producer, and these people, they're smarter than their predecessors, and they know the kind of sedative they need to tame the beast of their time, and they've done it. The only question for the beast is, how long does it plan to be knocked out? We're well past the century mark. So, what? Five hundred years, a thousand years? I can't control that. I can't face that kind of power. No one can. Not alone. What I can do is create pockets, and whoever enters those pockets, I can show them the good life and help them try to get their hands on it in a world where a set of rules exist to keep the boots of the bourgeoise on their throats, and a different set of rules help the bourgeoise get bigger boots every year to maintain the status quo."

Archibald crossed his hands over his chest as his facial expression continued to soften after his lengthy justification of his ways.

"I'm awake, my man, that's all I'm saying," said Archibald.

"That's powerful stuff," said Cornelius dryly. "We are all born with a strong internal narrator up here," he continued tapping his temple. "It's part of what helps us move past difficulties, embarrassments, disappointments, and guilt in our lives. Do you know why?"

Archibald's jaw stiffened slightly again. He knew what was coming, but that never helped. He shook his head.

"Because, no matter what our ego tells us, we're not alone in here," said Cornelius, tapping his finger against his temple with more force. "And that incessant narrator who weaves fantastic tales in your mind to convince you that you're worth a damn, that you should wake up tomorrow, is terrified of death. It will falsely reinvent you for as long as it takes so it can redeem its desires repeatedly through you. And anytime you fuckup your reinvention, it will tell you that it was a necessary outcome for an even greater reinvention until you are dry, stiff, and dead."

"Hey, man, listen," said Archibald, opening his arms.

"No, man, you listen," said Cornelius.

Shanice could feel the heat, and she could see the invisible flame a lick away from the fuse. She tucked her hand behind her back, slowly pulled the gun tucked into the back of her jeans and put it down softly on her lap.

"Our mother is dead; has been dead because of you. You knew where she came from. You knew that the people closest to her betrayed her trust, broke her heart, and ripped apart her spirit. You knew how long it took her to put herself back together, get away from those people, and build something of her own that she could count on to reflect her smile back onto her face. So, when you took from her what they took from her, she realized that even a life she created could do that to her, and if that was the case, it meant that there would never be anyone in this world she could trust, including herself. Because you were half of her. No, she saw us as all of her. You put that gun in her hand. You pressed the barrel against her temple, and you pulled that trigger even if you weren't in the room."

Archibald took a step back like he'd been shoved as tears coated his eyes. He put his fist over his mouth.

"All that articulation on the rise and fall of empires, the beast, the truth that's got your lady back there feeling you, you learned that from mom, you——"

Archibald lunged at Cornelius and grabbed him violently by the collar, liable to lift him off the ground if he put even an extra ounce of force into his grip. Cornelius glared at him, and Archibald knew it had more to do with his brother's now horribly wrinkled shirt than the force of the act. Archibald intentionally loosened his grip before quickly putting force back into it to wrinkle Cornelius' shirt even more to force his brother's hand.

Archibald's chest grew cold at the sound of a gun cocking.

"Baby, you know how I feel about blood putting hands on blood," said Shanice, sternly arching her head with her nostrils pointing at Archibald. "You know he's not going to put his hands on you, so stop trying."

Archibald let go of Cornelius' collar, and they both took a few steps back from each other. Shanice tucked her gun back beneath her leather jacket as Archibald cleared his throat.

"How's Nora?" asked Archibald.

"Jesus," said Shanice, looking down and shaking her head. "Does nobody in your family know how to apologize?"

"She's Nora. Anxious and overstimulated anytime there's more than three people in her sight."

Archibald chuckled, leaned over, and put his hands on his knees, facing the asphalt beneath his feet. This catchup session was knocking the wind out of his lungs.

Archibald stood straight again and silently walked up to Cornelius. He reached his hand out with wrinkles of remorse around his mouth and the corners of his eyes. Cornelius took his brother's hand and Archibald pulled him in for a hug, patting his back a few times before letting him go and walking back to the truck.

Cornelius cleared his throat with his hands behind his back and his gaze directed at his brother with a boyish timidity.

"When will we meet again?" asked Cornelius as his brother climbed up the side of the truck.

"Don't know," replied Archibald a bit coldly. "Don't forget, man. If you know anyone or see anyone who needs a bit of cash for food, a burner, a Wi-Fi hotspot, or less shitty clothes, give them my boy's number. He'll help them out... if you and everyone else can't be bothered."

Archibald, ever the pro of delivering the last jab, thought Cornelius. Letting it go wasn't a bother. The day would come when he'd be ready for it; to show his brother the depths of his feelings.

Shanice blew Cornelius a kiss and stepped away from the platform into the truck, and Archibald started to roll the door down, which was immediately followed by the sound of the truck's engine starting. The van covering the other side of the alleyway also started its engine prompting Cornelius to step out of the way and stand closer to the building.

Cornelius watched as the truck and van drove out of the alley towards Lakeside Drive. He stood there in silence with his shirt a mess of wrinkles. He looked down at his right hand with his palm facing out, as the shimmer of a sharp short dagger poked from beneath his sleeve. He reached across his chest over to his right shoulder with his left hand and clapped the side of his shoulder, which made a zipping sound as the dagger retracted.

He let out a frustrated exhale as he looked up at the sky with misery in his eyes. Archibald and Shanice didn't verbally announce it, but they were clearly expecting a child. He took in a frustrated inhale. He released his breath. He held his right palm up in front of his face, made a slight motion, and the dagger deployed back over his palm. He grimaced at his own reflection on the blade.

CHAPTER FIFTY-TWO

The car continued down the I-80 through West Wendover with Salt Lake City a whiff away. Mrs. Nelson yawned and rubbed her eyes as she awoke and looked back at Charles, still caught in his dreams, his head turned. She looked over at Lyla, who seemed to keep awake from the sheer will of getting them as far away from Berkeley as possible and closer to Cheyenne, despite the nearly seven-hour travel north still ahead of them before they'd reach the Cowboy State. Mrs. Nelson looked at a coffee cup inside another coffee cup resting in the cupholder. Lyla must've stopped at a diner between two and dawn when she'd fallen asleep. She pulled the lever and adjusted her chair upright again.

She put her hand on Lyla's shoulder. "You need to rest."

Lyla's eyes looked like a pair of pennies catching the morning light. She nodded. "We're ninety miles off the next rest stop." Mrs. Nelson's eyes widened. "I'll make it. Two hours out, no sweat." She looked at her and smiled.

The car zipped down the I-80 through Wendover and Lyla's limbs began to turn to Jell-O at the mere thought of the sweet relief ahead. If only to increase her odds of making it without snoozing off and veering into oblivion, she rolled down the window for the sting of fresh morning air to hustle the last remnants of energy out of her body.

She glanced for a moment at Mrs. Nelson, who'd dozed off again. The sound of a throttling engine drew Lyla's attention to her window where a bronze Chevy Malibu drove parallel to them.

"Eyes on the road you fucking dyke!" shouted a bald fellow from the passenger's seat, before Lyla flinched at the sight of a travel mug bouncing off the frame of the window and a warm spritz raining in. The Chevy raced away. The car skidded, momentarily waking Mrs. Nelson up before Lyla regained control.

"What—"

"Nothing, it's good. Everything is fine," said Lyla, feeling a warm buzz in her hands as she clutched the steering wheel tight. The car slowed down, and she made a U-turn.

They passed the Rest Stop sign and parked the car in front of the restrooms.

"Who was it?" asked Mrs. Nelson as Charles woke up. She wrapped Lyla's shaking hands in hers.

"No one. Just a prick with less sense than a coffee mug." She slowly pulled her hands away. "Go freshen up. I'll keep an eye on Charles. I'll go after."

Mrs. Nelson nodded and left the car. Lyla looked back at Charles.

"You hungry, sweetie?"

He nodded.

Lyla looked out the window at the vending machines a short walk away. She reached for the door handle, but her hand began to shake violently. Her heart raced. She pulled her hand away. She reached for the door handle again, but her hand jerked once more. She tried reaching for the door handle on the passenger's side, as though there was a spell on the one next to her, but her hand began to spasm. She looked back at Charles, trying to hold back her tears. She was a prisoner in her own car by some alternate will in her body, and she wasn't sure why.

A sharp echo rippled through her ears, causing her to cup her hands over them and whimper. She looked over at Charles, who seemed to shrink in his seat as he watched her.

Lyla grunted loudly as the pain in her ears grew sharper, seeming to burrow its way to her temple. The voice of the man in the Chevy Malibu echoed in her ears. She cried loudly again before falling completely silent.

Charles watched as Lyla's hands dropped from her ears and she looked at him like a different person; eyes hollowed, hands still but stiff, and her teeth sunk into her lips. She then looked at the glove compartment. She opened it and dug her hand into it, rummaging around.

She pulled a beige rectangular card out, then dropped it. She laughed the mad mumbling laugh of one who'd lost their mind and fallen into darkness.

Lyla picked the card up from the foot of her seat, put it on the dashboard, and rolled it up like a barbarian still learning to use their thumbs while trying to fashion out of it a rather sharp joint.

She continued to mumble nonsense. "You do, you do, you do… what's best… you. You do… what's best," she continued between her manic giggles.

She held the rolled-up card, looked at then away from Charles. She bit her lips, hyperventilated, and grunted as though hesitating, before letting out a cry and stabbing the sharp tubular card into her left ear with such force that blood passed through it in short, hesitant drips.

Charles held his breath and struggled to understand the lump of coal he felt growing in his chest as Lyla glared at him, half-herself and half a beast. She looked away and dug her hand back into the glove compartment. She shuffled through it for a moment before pulling out a gun.

Charles could feel his tears quietly running down his face as his lips quivered.

Mrs. Nelson stood in front of the mirror and felt herself lighter, her chest clear and tranquil, her heart beating to her own rhythm and not mirroring her husbands. Despite the sleep she'd had, she grew dizzy. She turned on the faucet and rinsed her face in cool water, each time closing her eyes and seeing Anson's body. The pollution seeped back into her heart again. She shut the faucet off and patted her face down with a grainy paper towel.

She looked at her reflection in the mirror, at her black turtleneck and her green skirt, how unsightly they were, how she wanted nothing more than to bundle them up and toss them in the trash. She looked at the ground. She'd forgotten her change of clothes in the car.

Nelson exited the restroom and walked toward the car with a smile on her face, before seeing a bright flash across the windshield, and hearing Charles scream.

The Chevy Malibu strolled into the rest stop and parked in the shaded parking spaces a short walk away from the restrooms.

"It's *tyke*. He said tyke," argued the marginally smaller of the two large, bald fellows.

Grayson sighed. "Mason, for fuck's sake, let it go. He said the trigger word was *dyke*. Now pass it." Mason passed him the binoculars.

"Why would it be dyke? It's tyke. Symbolic, isn't it? Cause she's got the kid." Mason looked at Grayson, who watched him like one bemused by a monkey playing with a banana peel.

"It's dyke, cause they're fucking dykes, you idiot! Jesus, we're lucky Ma isn't around, or she'd make us lick the pavement until we promised not to repeat that word again."

"Okay," said Mason, pulling a crisp Benjamin from his pocket and slapping it down on the dashboard. "Should be what, five, ten minutes? If it gets loud, it's yours. If it stays quiet, you get to be Ma's mall-bitch for a month. See how you like trying to convince her she doesn't need a G-string without a man in her life, and not make her cry."

Grayson smiled.

"Smile all you want. I know Mr. Dillinger better than you do. I've seen him do his hypnosis shit firsthand. I know his suggestions better. I know the triggers he likes to use better. He's a poet. He's not about to use dy—" Mason flinched as a loud shot echoed. "Fuck!"

Grayson chuckled, put the binoculars down and pocketed the bill.

The two of them got out of the car and watched as Mrs. Nelson ran from the bathroom toward the BMW, the windshield red with Lyla's brain.

Mrs. Nelson opened the driver's side door, looked in the car, then dropped to her knees and vomited. She put her hand over her stomach and forced herself quickly onto her feet as she wiped her mouth with her sleeve. She opened the backseat door and frantically wrestled with the buckle before freeing Charles and pulling him out. She kept him shielded behind the door, then returned to Lyla and what remained of her head.

She pressed her hands over her mouth but couldn't stop her tears or the sound of her crying from leaking uncontrollably. She shifted a few steps away as the gun slipped from Lyla's hand and out onto the concrete. She noticed something rolled up and stuffed in Lyla's ear and upon closer examination, she realized what it was.

The Twizzler-red borders gave it away.

Mrs. Nelson turned quickly to Charles, but he was no longer behind the backseat door. Rather, he was sitting on the car trunk, high fiving a large bald fellow.

"Annabelle, baby." Grayson looked at her with enthused welcome as she turned around and watched five meaty knuckles flying at her face.

CHAPTER FIFTY-THREE

A large, broad-shouldered man entered the hallway, his mammoth steps eclipsing every tile he passed over. He wore a light-blue button-up tucked into a pair of navy trousers, with brown suspenders looping over his shoulders, and hefty leather shoes that could stomp straight through a sewer grate.

He approached Wish as she sat on the bench outside the lab doors.

"Captain," she said without averting her eyes from the floor.

"You good?" He continued to suck on his cherry flavored candy while unwrapping another. She nodded. He squatted and buried her knees under his hands. "Any other day, and you know I'd send you home, but today—"

Wish looked at him. "What happened?" She wiped a tear from under her eye; the sight of Anson's cold corpse still flashing through her mind.

He sighed. "Got two more crime scenes on our hands, we think."

"We think?"

"One, down by the public library on Kittredge. Coffee shop next door. Manager came in at dawn, found his closer from yesterday dead on the ground with a funnel jammed down his throat." He brushed his finger up and down his throat. "Thinking it's drugs. Boy forgot he was in a coffee shop, stuffed a funnel down his throat, skipped the coffee beans, and poured bleach down his throat."

Wish felt dizzy just thinking about what had to be the most twisted method of saying goodbye to the world she'd ever heard of.

"He must've been on some special goo. Then we got a Bart uniform downtown trying to wax on, wax off the Fremont train while it was still incoming. Worse yet, he lives right across the street from vic one." The Captain pointed his thumb over his shoulder at the lab doors where Mr. Nelson's stiff corpse rested. "And we don't know if he had anything to do with the double homicide down on fifty-sixth street, or if he was on the same shit the barista was. Plus, the wife and child of…" He pulled his notepad out of his pocket and flipped through it. "Mr. Nelson, are missing."

He stood up, reached his hand out, and helped her up. "So, I hear it's your neighbor in there? Mr. Green looks like he's got this here, and Kevin's at the coffee shop, so I need you down at Bart. You up for this?"

"Fuck yes," said Wish, feeling energized by a boiling rage in her veins.

"That's what I like to hear." He reached into his pocket and pulled out his keys. "Take the car and get going." She took the keys.

"Captain Harshdinger, Captain Harshdinger," said a voice a few feet away as a reporter approached him.

"Aye!" he shouted at the uniform down the hallway and pointed at the reporter. The uniform dropped his coffee and raced towards her. "You know what a reporter looks like, son?!" he shouted as the officer led the reporter away. "Somebody, mop that up." He pointed at the puddle of coffee.

"Cornelius is back in town," said Wish suddenly before heading past him down the hallway.

"Where?" he asked, stopping her at the exit.

"Claremont. I'll text you his address. You should talk."

Captain Harshdinger smiled and Wish left. He pulled his wallet from his pocket, took out an old, wrinkled photo, stared at it for a moment before tucking it back in and heading into the lab.

CHAPTER FIFTY-FOUR

Dr. Heller's phone buzzed. She opened the attachment sent to her from Salwa. It seemed Ma was not perturbed by the passing of Mr. Dillinger and the termination of Mr. Karpis, as her other lackeys continued to roam her den. She closed the photo and sent her a reply.

Knocks sounded from the door.

"Come in," she said, looking down at her phone and reopening Rahma's message.

At least she was now certain that Rahma was okay, after a sleepless night pondering why she hadn't sent any updates from the Oakland burners. Just as the door slowly opened, she received an attachment from Rahma. She put her phone away.

Nora poked her head in, then entered with a paper in her hand that read, *please knock.*

"Welcome. I'm so glad you're finally here." She got up from her desk and approached Nora. "So sorry about yesterday. It became overwhelming very quickly, and I wanted to be sure our consultation went as smoothly as possible." She took the paper from Nora, balled it up and shot it into the bin by her desk. "Please sit."

Dr. Heller sat down, and Nora got comfortable on the couch.

"Again, sorry about yesterday." She waited to see if Nora would apologize for Saturday's mess, but no apology seemed imminent.

Nora reached into her pocket for her pen and notepad.

"Actually," said the doctor, "I was hoping you could use this." She pulled a sixteen by twenty-four-inch whiteboard and a black marker from her side and put them on the coffee table. "My eyesight isn't what it used to be."

Nora looked at the whiteboard, then at her hand stuffed in her pocket, before looking back at the whiteboard. She pulled her hand out and grabbed the board and marker.

"Thanks for understanding."

Nora nodded with the most microscopic of smiles.

"Well then, if you don't mind me asking, why the hesitation? Why have you resisted a consultation all this time? You must have noticed the strain it's put on Cornelius."

Dr. Heller examined Nora with a surgical stare. Be it the look in Nora's eyes, all the research she'd done into her past, or the videos she'd reviewed of her and Cornelius in the units, she knew this would prove an entirely different undertaking to what usually worked with her other clients.

Control, Nora scribbled onto the board and pointed it at her.

"You mean the cameras? I assure you, it's only to review the client's progress. Any hesitation or escalation in what they do in my units helps me strategize my approach for our next session. I am not holding anything over anyone's head, which is why I encourage you to never take off your mask and to adhere to the strict dress code. If I'm ever taken in, you can rest assured it will be in a body bag, and everything will be destroyed well before I draw my last breath. I've spent a decade putting all this together so that I can better help people like you who the system would otherwise simply toss in a cell."

Nelly says that you do not charge your clients. What's in it for you?

Dr. Heller pondered for a moment. She didn't want this to turn into an interrogation. To unfold her entire operation to Nora would take several sessions—not that she intended to. The session was intended for her to learn more about Nora and hopefully convince her to return. "There are a lot of people out there. From what Cornelius tells me, you feel that more severely than most."

Nora nodded.

"Okay, let me put it this way. Vultures, sharks, and wolves are often wrongly perceived as ominous and vicious creatures because of how they look, how they react, and how they stalk. Are they though? No. Vultures scavenge carcasses to prevent the spread of disease. Sharks regulate populations of marine species to balance the ecosystems of oceans. Wolves help control the population of prey species to prevent overgrazing and ecosystem imbalance."

Nora's smile grew less contained.

"What I see in my clients is an energy that can be put to better use in our societal ecosystem than sitting behind bars. There are a lot of diseased over-grazers out there, and they come packaged in every which way you can imagine. Privileged, middling, and impoverished, but they all have the same itch no matter where they start and where they end up, and that is to exploit without prejudice until they feel satiated, and that, young lady, creates a buildup of negative imbalance."

Dr. Heller hunched over and pushed the manila folder on the coffee table toward her. Nora looked at her, the doctor nodded, then she picked it up.

"Nora. You are a vulture, you are a shark, and you are a wolf, and you are not bad. You do not have the urge you have because it is fun, or because it enriches you or strokes your ego, but because of a deeply engrained coding to right what is wrong in the world. That is why you belong out here, and why the likes of Ted Bundy, and Dorothy Puente belonged behind bars. However, make no mistake, if you practice your urge for too long, you will eventually do it for the wrong reasons. I've witnessed it happen before, and I don't want to see it happen to anyone ever again."

Dr. Heller nodded at the folder in Nora's hand.

Nora opened it. A green-eyed, graying fella looked back at her with a smile on his face, as he, and perhaps his daughter, held up a fish they'd just caught for the camera. She looked at the doctor with concern.

"Don't let this worry you. I don't keep files on my clients. The best trail is no trail. All I have are my notes and my client's aliases. I've got to track their progress somehow, but it's all shorthand and it means shit to anyone who isn't me." Dr. Heller smiled and nodded at the folder. "I put that together just for you, just for today. The photo is from his Facebook page."

Nora unclipped the photo, set it aside, and flipped through the pages.

"Mr. McClure was a client of mine. May he rest in peace."

She continued to read.

"Five years ago, his daughter took her own life. The young girl wasn't about to open for Valentino, and neither would most kids her age anywhere, but unlike most of the kids her age, her lack of perfect symmetry and cover-worthy lips didn't drive her up a wall. She was bright and kind, dressed up every day, put a smile on her face, and tried to be a kid. Tried to blend in, and make friends. But you know, some people don't like that. They don't like it when you're happier than they are, and they don't see why anyone else besides them should be. Why someone who doesn't look like them, walk like them, smell like them, and command attention like them, ought to be."

Nora looked up from the folder.

"She tried, but she couldn't take it anymore. The moment she left home, she walked into a jungle. The bus, her classrooms, recess, the bathroom; every place was a minefield of cruel youth; a prank waiting to put her down, to put her in her place."

Dr. Heller crossed her legs. "When he lost her, Mr. McClure had only one thing in mind. 'Squeeze the life out of every last one of those little things.' But he had a wife who loved him, brothers and sisters who cherished him, and a mother who'd miss him. That's where I come in. Tell me, Nora, how many people do you think go missing every year?" she asked.

Nora put the folder down and scribbled on the whiteboard. *Not enough.*

Dr. Heller held her breath, fearing she'd welcomed the second coming of Countess Elizabeth Báthory into her office, much less Dorothy Puente, but she understood from her audit of Nora's past that this was farthest from the truth.

"Hundreds of thousands," she continued, "and very few are ever found. More people go missing than there is staffing to handle those cases. They find themselves at the bottom of the stack beneath homicides, attempted homicides, and assaults, vying for attention with the rest. This puts my clients at a remarkable advantage with the environment and scheme I provide them with to exercise their urges."

Nora shook her head with a smile. She wrote on the board then held it up.

That is a lie. Out of almost 800,000 missing persons cases a year, almost 99% of them are solved.

"I apologize for the deception," said Dr. Heller with a chuckle and a smile. "I know you and Cornelius work together in the same field, so I assumed you were very intelligent, but life has taught me to test my assumptions if I want to avoid regret. My line of work allows for zero clumsiness and absentmindedness from myself and my clients."

The room went completely dark. Nora didn't flinch as a short buzzing sound came from the ceiling before green rays of light projected hundreds if not thousands of green rectangles across every wall and surface in the office.

"I'll tell you something, young lady. With the amount of funds and resource misappropriation that Uncle Sam propagates, there isn't a prayer in this world that law enforcement agencies have faultless numbers, if even numbers with moderately acceptable margins of error."

Nora got up and walked closer to the wall by the door. She brought her face closer to the wall and saw that the rectangles framed faces. She looked at Dr. Heller with feral eyes. Dr. Heller knew exactly what Nora wanted to know without needing her to write it down.

"You can assume that most of them are dead," Dr. Heller said with the hairs on her neck standing at Nora's eyes fixed on her.

The room went dark, then the lights on the ceiling switched back on.

"Please, sit," she pointed at the couch hoping Nora would sit down and calm her excitement rather than pounce on her. She heard a squeaking sound with Nora's face now turned back to the wall.

Nora turned around and stepped away from the wall.

You don't understand. She wrote with a permanent marker on the wall.

Dr. Heller understood that Nora was testing her temperament. She clearly wasn't going to make any part of their potential partnership easy. What Dr. Heller considered critical was figuring out if Nora's intention was to lure her in so she could sabotage her and eliminate her from Cornelius' life, or if it was simply a matter of Nora holding the assumption that she was remarkably resourceful and intelligent in guiding her clients, and she just wanted to test that assumption.

Nora's face calmed and she sat back down on the couch.

Dr. Heller got up, went to her desk, opened a drawer, and returned with three things: a sheet of paper, a bottle of black pepper, and a small glass bowl filled with sugar cubes. She hunched over and put the paper down at the center of the table. She twisted the lid off the bottle, carefully poured a small heap of black peppercorns on the sheet, then spread them around. She put the bottle down, then removed the tong from the side of the sugar bowl and picked one cube at a time until she'd set down five sugar cubes on the paper, huddled next to each other. She then put the bottle and bowl down on the ground by the table and out of sight.

She looked up at Nora. "Am I close?"

Nora nodded. She felt something welling up in her chest— joy?

The doctor examined the paper carefully, then looked back at Nora, who'd been glancing at the sugar cubes with a fond smile.

Dr. Heller grinned. She grabbed all but one of the cubes, sucked them down one by one a little until they were damp and shrunk somewhat, before placing them back on the paper around the perfect dry cube.

She looked up at Nora, who'd suddenly brandished a wide smile that banished the aloofness she entered the room with.

"I know you love Cornelius, Mr. Harshdinger, the late Mrs. Harshdinger, Wish, and your brother—wherever he may be, whatever he's doing—and I know you'd like us to see the world in the same way. However, I need you to understand something. To say that you want all those people out there gone, it's not how you truly feel. I don't believe that."

Nora sat back; her smile gone from her face like a sickle entombed into sodden earth.

Dr. Heller felt like a gecko on a branch, darting its eyes nervously as a serpentine hiss drew nearer. "What I mean to say is there are plenty of dark seeds out there, many people with a dark flame waiting to be snuffed, but it's not all of them. I know what you're afraid of. I know what your mother and father did to you. Tell me about them. How they were when the world couldn't see them? When God watched them but did nothing, and I promise I'll lead you to just the type of people who were born to suffer your hurt. To feel your rage." Dr. Heller sat back and watched as Nora looked at the whiteboard with reluctance before grabbing the marker.

"No, wait."

Dr. Heller went to her desk, kneeled by the printer, opened the tray, and returned to Nora with a stack of papers and a cup filled with pens.

CHAPTER FIFTY-FIVE

Mr. Dillinger and Ms. Karpis stood at the corner of Sacramento and Alcatraz and watched the squad car parked in front of Nelson's shop. Mr. Dillinger sighed.

Ms. Karpis looked at him. "What?"

"Ma's not going to be in a good mood," he said.

"Any evidence in there?" she asked.

"Not a shred, but she hates messes. Leaving his murder to his lady will likely prove a regret no matter how fed up Ma was with him. Mr. Nelson had to go, but she will perhaps wonder if there was an equally organic way for her to be done with him without all this grime. Going to take a year or two before we're able to set up shop again in Berkeley, maybe three. Going to have to get another one of her girls and a new Mr. Nelson down here, or probably ditch the name for the best and call them the Hamiltons or something." Mr. Dillinger peeked from the corner of his eyes but struggled to see her clearly. "Is Salwa still following us?" he whispered.

"Like a fucking cucaracha," Ms. Karpis said. "How did she know we were even here? Didn't Ma only sign-in Shaw and Warwell with the Proselyte?"

It sounded like he'd been wheezing before she realized he'd only been laughing deeply. "Thank you, dear, for scaring the clouds away." He wiped a tear from his eye. Ms. Karpis stabbed her brow at him. "It's something you'd have learned soon enough but let me tell you now. Ma and the Proselyte, the breadth of their intellect is not something that comes along too often. They fancy themselves modern-day Sherlock Holmes', just with opposite intentions upon society. The two of them use the homeless network quite extensively, just as he did in those stories." He walked away from Sacramento down Alcatraz and Ms. Karpis followed.

"Still, it's not like she could've known which of us Ma was going to send in on the down low. We're not the only ones at her disposal."

"She doesn't need to," said Mr. Dillinger. "The Proselyte is quite educated in how Ma runs things and who she chooses to do what. Don't forget, there was once a time they ran The Town together before their big divide. Well before your time."

"So, what, the homeless can just sniff us out?" she asked.

They continued down Alcatraz toward King. "Not quite. If anything, they've been conditioned to understand our movements. Our pairings, our chemistry, our gaze, our general areas of interest. The stupid pink raincoats some of us wear. Is she still following us?" he asked under his breath.

They both stopped just a few feet away from King Street, where Salwa suddenly reappeared. They looked back and wondered when the hell she'd rounded them. They turned their attention to her. Despite her small frame, she stood before them like a wall wearing a gray, white and teal headscarf.

"You're up, Mr. Saggy. There's a Dodge pickup two blocks back. How about you suggest puta take a close look at its shiny bumper?"

Mr. Dillinger sighed. "It's not moving fast enough, and they'll probably just hit the brakes. If it was midnight instead of noon, and a weekend instead of a Monday, then it'd probably be fifty-fifty if the driver's a drunkard and I can get a jump on her."

"Fine then." Ms. Karpis tucked her hand into the deep pocket of her raincoat and grabbed the shiv that used to be her father's toothbrush.

He grabbed her by the wrist. "I'd think twice about that, deary. Since she's here, and the Proselyte is aware of our presence, then we may just have woken the den."

She looked up at him as he shot his eyes at their surroundings warily, as if any and every passerby was an agent of the Proselyte, then loosened his grip.

The two of them approached Salwa and stopped six feet away.

"Salam, Salwa, it's been such a long time. How's Rahma doing? Not worried about you being out here all alone? It may be Berkeley, but you never know whether a racist or a misogynistic fundamentalist may be lurking just around the corner." Mr. Dillinger held her gaze. She remained stoic and unflinching without reply. "We're actually leaving. Just heading down to Ashby, by the way. Should catch the Millbrae train out on time."

Salwa shook her head and gestured them over, before turning around, looking both ways and crossing the street. They both followed her, Mr. Dillinger a little too obediently for Ms. Karpis' liking.

"Are we seriously getting escorted to Bart by Napoleon's bebita?" asked Ms. Karpis, looking at Mr. Dillinger, who remained silent. "Dios mío, whatever. You're such a wuss."

CHAPTER FIFTY-SIX

Joseph straightened his tie, eyed his suit, then stepped back. This was better. Less brown; navy-blue was a winner. He could sell a rock on rolling pins if he had to. He got out of the bathroom, grabbed his bag, made sure his phone was in his pocket, and stepped out.

He locked the door and found himself facing a large fellow exiting Anson's place, wearing a similarly navy suit with less fit and more flow to it.

"Good morning. Are you?" The large fellow pulled a notepad from his pocket and flipped through it. "Joseph Fulton?"

"Yeah, that's me. Everything alright, sir?" His heart began to race.

"Unfortunately, not. Everything's messy right now." The man extended his hand to Joseph. "Captain Walter Harshdinger of the BPD. If you don't mind, I've got a few questions for you about the late Mr. Anson Smith."

Joseph shook his hand with some hesitation. "It's my first day at my new job. Can't be late. This is tragic, but can we do this later today? Maybe drop by the dealership during my lunch?" he asked, immediately feeling silly for asking.

Their hands parted and Captain Harshdinger shook his head. "That won't be possible, son. Chasing some leads that are time sensitive. Anything you can tell us will be a huge help. Sergeant!" he called, and a uniform exited the apartment and joined them. "Tell him where you work, and he'll call in for you."

Joseph opened his locker, tucked in his bag, and turned to the sight of Jim's nose poking at him.

"You okay, son?" he said, leaning back. "That call was grim. Was afraid we lost you."

"Yeah, I'm fine. Looks like my neighbor was one-half of a homicide down on fifty-sixth."

"Jesus, that's tough. You knew the guy?" Jim gestured for him to follow over to the table.

"Not much," he said as they sat in the break room. "I've only been in town since Wednesday night. Haven't made too many friends yet, but I had a brief chat with him yesterday. Looked excited, said he met someone. Turns out she was married, and both he and her husband got into it. BPD is still trying to figure it out."

"Poor guy. Probably didn't even know she was married, or maybe he was a sleaze. Love can turn shit upside down quick if you're not careful." He frowned. "You okay to work today? Knew him or not, death that close to your doorstep can't be easy."

"Yeah, I'm fine. I've got a proper suit." Joseph smiled and brushed his fingers over his shoulders. "I'm ready to sell some cars."

"Alright." Jim slapped his hand down on the table. "Good man. Go get that bacon." They both got up and walked side by side out to the gallery. "Death aside, your weekend was good?"

Joseph wanted to fall to the ground and laugh manically at that question, but he'd have to wait until he got home and closed the door.

"Weekend was great," said Joseph as Jim patted his shoulder then entered his office.

The gallery was empty, but for a tall young man with curly hair standing in front of the Fusion Hybrid while seeming more preoccupied with his collar and the hem of his T-shirt. "Good morning, sir. Do I assume correctly that you're in the market for a car?" Joseph smiled.

The young man looked up and returned his smile. "Yes. Not for me, though, but for a friend."

"That's generous of you. Let me help you figure out what they might like. Joseph, by the way."

"Cornelius."

They shook hands.

"So, tell me about this friend of yours. What are they like?"

"She's an artist."

ABOUT THE AUTHOR

Medo H. Maz is the pen name of Ahmed Al-Maznai. His passion for writing began in Sana'a, Yemen, more than a decade ago. He started by crafting numerous proverbs, which later evolved into composing poetry, followed by short stories, and eventually culminating in several novels. Medo enjoys delving into an eclectic range of fiction and non-fiction, ranging from Odd Thomas to Between the World and Me. He loves cats, is a loyal and frequently miserable Manchester United supporter, a chocolate and sugary-treats seeker, and a social-media-averse old soul. He lives in Berkeley.

www.medomaz.com

Thanks for reading my book! If you have any time to spare to leave a review, it'd be hugely appreciated!

www.ingramcontent.com/pod-product-compliance
Lightning Source LLC
Chambersburg PA
CBHW072112300726
48975CB00003B/785